DON'T GIVE UP,
MALLORY

**Other books by
Ann M. Martin**

Leo the Magnificat
Rachel Parker, Kindergarten Show-off
Eleven Kids, One Summer
Ma and Pa Dracula
Yours Turly, Shirley
Ten Kids, No Pets
Slam Book
Just a Summer Romance
Missing Since Monday
With You and Without You
Me and Katie (the Pest)
Stage Fright
Inside Out
Bummer Summer

THE KIDS IN MS. COLMAN'S CLASS series
BABY-SITTERS LITTLE SISTER series
THE BABY-SITTERS CLUB mysteries
THE BABY-SITTERS CLUB series

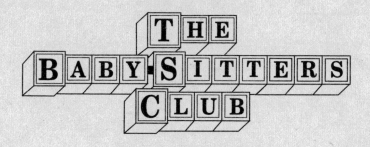

DON'T GIVE UP, MALLORY

Ann M. Martin

AN
APPLE
PAPERBACK

SCHOLASTIC INC.
New York Toronto London Auckland Sydney

Cover art by Hodges Soileau

ISBN 0-590-69214-3

12 11 10 9 8 7 6 5 4 3 2 1   7 8 9/9 0 1 2/0

Printed in the U.S.A.   40

First Scholastic printing, May 1997

*The author gratefully acknowledges
Jahnna Beecham and Malcolm Hillgartner
for their help in
preparing this manuscript.*

DON'T GIVE UP, MALLORY

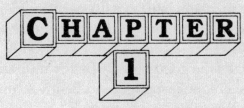

CHAPTER 1

"All right, class," Mrs. Frederickson announced to my homeroom. "I've got good news and bad news."

"Tell us the bad news first," Benny Ott called from the back of the class. "Get it over with."

Mrs. Frederickson waved the stack of computer printouts in her hand. "It's time for midterm progress reports."

"Oh, no!" A groan circled the room, like one of those stadium waves you see at a baseball or football game.

I was one of the few who didn't groan. I knew my grades would be good. Well, actually, better than good. I don't want to brag or anything, but I'm an excellent student.

Who am I? Mallory Pike. Mal to my friends. I'm eleven years old and live in Stoneybrook, Connecticut. And I'm a sixth-grader at Stoneybrook Middle School.

"What's the good news?" Rachel Robinson asked, from her desk in front of me.

"The good news is, this is only a progress report," Mrs. Frederickson said. "It's not your final grade. You still have nearly a month to work hard and bring up your scores if you need to."

"That's the good news?" Benny muttered.

Mrs. Frederickson ignored Benny's comment and began calling our names.

"Mallory Pike." Mrs. Frederickson waved my report in the air. I left my desk in the third row and walked to the front of the room.

Mrs. Frederickson smiled over the top of her glasses. "Congratulations, Mallory. You should be very proud."

I smiled back as I reached for my midterm report. The piece of paper slipped through my fingers and wafted to the floor between Randy Rademacher and Laura Nelson.

Randy's eyes nearly bugged out of his head as he gasped, "Straight A's? What a brainiac!"

That wave thing happened again. Only this time everyone was staring at me and repeating, "Straight A's!"

"She thinks she's so smart," Janet O'Neal whispered across the aisle behind me. "Miss Know-it-all!"

That did it. First the tips of my ears turned

red. Then my cheeks. Then my freckles lit up. In an instant my whole face was glowing.

I squeezed my eyes shut and made a secret wish for the floor to open up and swallow me. (It didn't.) I had to pick up my report and walk stiffly back to my desk.

Luckily, my best friend, Jessica Ramsey, was there to support me. She patted me on the shoulder and whispered, "All right, Mal!"

I thanked her, then slumped down in my seat and stared at my report. I knew my parents would be proud of me. But they're proud of all the kids in my family. There are eight of us. Yes, eight!

People call us stair-step kids because we were born one right after the other. First there's me, then Byron, Adam, and Jordan, who are ten. They're identical triplets.

Then comes Vanessa, who's nine. She's our dreamy poet, and she is the slowest person on the planet. Mom has to wake Vanessa twenty minutes before everyone else, because it takes her so long to get dressed.

Nicky, eight, is a ball of energy. He likes softball, hates girls, and is a champion hider.

Margo is seven. She's the reason barf bags were invented. She gets carsick, airsick — Margo even throws up on merry-go-rounds.

And last but not least, there's Claire, who's

five. She can be lovable and huggable one second, and the queen of temper tantrums the next.

Mom and Dad bring the Pike total to ten. Can you imagine what our family vacations are like? They're nuts. We have to take two cars.

Most of us Pikes have blue eyes and chestnut-colored hair. I'm the only one whose hair is reddish and curly. I'm also the only one with braces. (Lucky me.) I have pierced ears, because I *finally* convinced my parents to let me get them pierced. But I wear glasses, and I have to wait until I'm fifteen to wear contacts.

I'm hardworking and very responsible. For as long as I can remember, I've helped Mom and Dad take care of my brothers and sisters. I started out as an unpaid mother's helper but soon advanced to paid baby-sitter. I even became a member of the BSC (Baby-sitters Club). But I'll tell you about that later.

The greatest moment in my life: winning the Young Author's Day Award for Best Overall Fiction at my school.

The worst moment: coming down with mononucleosis and having to quit the Baby-sitters Club temporarily. (I'm back in it now.)

I like studying. And I like earning good grades. I just don't necessarily like the whole school to know about it. But, boy, does word travel fast.

Jessi and I were on our way to second period English when Nan White and Rachel Robinson shouted, "There she is — Mallory Pike, Miss Know-it-all!"

"Ignore those guys," Jessi whispered, looping her arm through mine. "They're just jealous."

Jessi knows what it's like to be teased. When she first moved to Stoneybrook, some people made fun of her just because she was the only black student in sixth grade. Isn't that stupid?

Luckily, that's changed. Jessi and her family — her sister, Becca (short for Rebecca), and baby brother, Squirt (John Philip Ramsey, Jr.), her mom and dad, and her Aunt Cecelia — are very happy here now.

Jessi, who has gorgeous long legs and graceful arms, dreams of becoming a famous ballerina. And I'm sure she will. She is a star student at her dancing school in Stamford and has already danced the lead in several productions, including the ballet *Coppélia*.

Jessi and I have a lot in common. We absolutely love horse books, especially ones written by Marguerite Henry. We also love kids, and we're junior officers in the Baby-sitters Club. We both think Benny Ott can be a major pain. Especially today.

"Straight A's, huh, Mallory?" Benny said, shoving his face in between Jessi and me as we

5

made our way down the hall. "I could do that, if I cared."

"Yeah, right, Benny," Jessi shot back.

Benny crossed his eyes and made his standard goon face.

I would have laughed, but too many people were teasing me about my grades.

Jessi and I had reached the door to Mr. Williams's class, when someone else grabbed my arm.

"Oh, great," I thought. "Not another one."

Luckily it was Justin Price, president of the sixth grade.

"Yo, Mallory, don't forget about fund-raising week," he said. "It's just around the corner."

"How could I forget?" I replied. "I'm in charge of all the booths."

Justin grinned his "cutest boy in sixth grade" grin and said, "I know you wouldn't forget. I just want to make sure you have things under control."

Sixth-grade fund-raising week has always been a major event at SMS. The money each class raises goes to help the school or students in some way.

As sixth-grade class secretary, I'd spent the entire month of April working with my committee and organizing the event. We planned to hold a different fund-raiser each day of the school week.

"The booths are ready to go," I said. "Any more thoughts on what we should do with our donation?"

Justin pushed his blond hair off his forehead. "That's still up in the air."

"We'd better decide pretty soon," I reminded him. "It's already the beginning of May."

"Let's contact the rest of the officers and arrange a meeting to talk about this." Justin checked the calendar that he kept at the front of his notebook. "How does next Thursday sound?"

"Great. I'll make the calls," I said, putting my hand on the doorknob to Mr. Williams's room.

By now the halls were starting to empty. I knew that I had only a few more seconds before I would be tardy.

"I'll let you know if everyone can make it," I said, flinging open the door to Mr. Williams's English class and scooting inside just as the bell rang.

I took my seat and looked up at my teacher. Mr. Williams stood by the blackboard with his hands resting on top of his little potbelly, a broad grin on his round face.

"Mr. Kingbridge has announced the next round of Short Takes classes," Mr. Williams declared. "Naturally, you won't all be in the same Short Takes groups, but you will study the same subject."

I love the Short Takes program. For several weeks at a time, everybody at SMS studies one subject intensively. It's usually a subject that regular classes don't cover.

"I know many of you in this room are going to like this one." Mr. Williams stepped away from the board to reveal the title of the next course. "Children's literature," he said with a grin. "This course is one of my favorites."

"Hooray!" I squealed.

Several of the kids turned in their seats and laughed at me, but it was good-natured. They knew that I plan to be a children's book author and illustrator when I grow up.

"Some very dynamic teachers will be teaching this unit," he explained, "including Mr. Cobb, Mrs. Simon, and Ms. Garcia."

"Damien Cobb?" Maria Fazio whispered from across the aisle. "I hope I'm in his class. He is so cool."

Mr. Cobb is one of the newest teachers at SMS. And Maria was right. He *is* cool. He's also handsome and young. He graduated from Princeton last year. Just thinking about having him for a teacher made my heart thump a little faster.

"In your classes, you will be analyzing children's literature, focusing particularly on illustrated books."

I didn't squeal this time. But I wanted to.

Could anything be more fun than analyzing picture books?

I felt a tap on my shoulder. It was Jessi. "Happy?" she whispered into my ear.

I grinned and nodded. "I'm ecstatic."

Mr. Williams explained that the class would begin Monday. "At that time you will receive the list of books to be read and discussed during the course."

Monday was only three days away. I could hardly wait.

The rest of the day went by in a blur. I forgot about my progress report or being teased about my good grades. All I could think about was spending the next few weeks studying children's literature with Mr. Cobb. Heaven!

When I went home that Friday afternoon, I wasn't walking — I was floating.

CHAPTER 2

"It's nearly five-thirty," Vanessa said, sticking her head in our bedroom later that afternoon. "Don't you have a BSC meeting today?"

I looked at my alarm clock. 5:27. "Yikes!"

I'd spent the last couple of hours in my room, rereading children's picture books and daydreaming about the Short Takes class that would begin on Monday. I'd spaced on the Baby-sitters Club meeting. Which is something you never *ever* want to do.

Why? Because Kristy Thomas, our president, hates latecomers.

"Look out!" I yelled as I bolted past my sister into the hall. I ran down the stairs three at a time. In a flash I was out the door and on my bike.

I checked my watch. Two minutes to pedal a few blocks to Claudia Kishi's house. Could I make it? I was going to try.

There are seven of us in the club, nine if you

count associate members, ten if you include our honorary member. But there weren't always that many of us.

In the beginning (this sounds really formal, doesn't it?). *In the beginning* . . . there was Kristy. Back then, she lived on Bradford Court across the street from Claudia. Mrs. Thomas was a divorced, working mom trying to raise four kids by herself. Kristy helped out as much as she could by looking after her younger brother, David Michael. But one particular afternoon, Kristy wasn't available to baby-sit, and neither were her two older brothers. She listened to her mom make phone call after phone call trying to find a sitter.

That's when the brilliant idea hit Kristy. *Why not form a club?* she thought. A baby-sitters club. Then parents could call one number and reach a lot of sitters.

Kristy talked to her best friend and next-door neighbor, Mary Anne Spier. Then they talked to Claudia Kishi, who talked to Stacey McGill — and presto! The Baby-sitters Club was formed.

Luckily for me, the club was an instant success, and the girls had to bring in more members. Dawn Schafer was the next to join. Then came Jessi and me. Last, but definitely not least, Abby Stevenson joined us. Dawn has since moved back to California, so that brings our current number of regular members to seven.

We meet for half an hour, from five-thirty until six, every Monday, Wednesday, and Friday in Claudia's room. During that time, we catch up on gossip, eat junk food (courtesy of Claud), and, most important, take clients' calls. And boy, do they call. Some days the phone doesn't stop ringing during the entire thirty minutes.

In fact, when I arrived at Claudia's, I could hear the phone ringing upstairs. I dropped my bike in the driveway and charged through the front door and straight up the stairs to Claud's room. I was winded and pouring sweat.

"Baby-sitters Club," Kristy chirped into the phone. She caught sight of me bent over in the doorway, trying to catch my breath, and arched one eyebrow.

I mouthed, "Sorry," to her, then staggered to my usual spot, next to Jessi at the foot of Claud's bed.

"Hi, Mrs. DeWitt," Kristy said into the phone. She was still watching me as I tried to wipe the sweat off my face with the bottom of my T-shirt. The corners of her mouth curled up in a smile and I relaxed.

Good. Kristy wasn't mad.

Kristy can be a pretty strict leader. Some people might even call her bossy, but that's what makes her such a good president. She's the glue that keeps us together, despite the fact that her personal life has been pretty topsy-turvy.

First her dad walked out on her mom, leaving Mrs. Thomas with four kids: Charlie and Sam, who are both in high school now; Kristy, who is an eighth-grader; and seven-year-old David Michael. Kristy's mom had to struggle for a long while. But then Watson Brewer came into their lives, and nothing was the same again.

Watson is — are you ready for this? — a millionaire. He and Kristy's mom fell in love and wham: Kristy went from living in a nice little house on Bradford Court to this incredibly huge mansion across town on McLelland Road. And that wasn't the only thing that changed.

Their family grew bigger and bigger. You see, Watson has two kids from his first marriage — Andrew, who's four, and Karen, who's seven. Then Watson and Mrs. Brewer decided to adopt Emily Michelle, a toddler who was born in Vietnam. During the months Karen and Andrew live at Watson's house (they alternate), there are seven kids around (almost as many as in my family). Luckily for them, Kristy's grandmother, Nannie, moved in to help take care of Emily Michelle (and everyone else).

Besides being our president and the main

idea person behind all of our great events, Kristy is the coach of Kristy's Krushers, a softball team she formed for some of our younger charges. You'd think such a powerhouse person would be tall. But she isn't. She's the shortest girl in the eighth grade.

No one would ever mistake Kristy for a clotheshorse, either. Kristy's standard uniform is jeans, a sweatshirt, and a baseball cap pulled over her shoulder-length brown hair.

"Two sitters for the Barrett-DeWitts next Wednesday at six-thirty," Kristy called to Mary Anne after she hung up the phone. "Who's available?"

Mary Anne ran her finger down the calendar in the BSC record book and said, "Stacey and Claud, your schedules are clear. Do you want to take this one?"

Stacey gave Mary Anne a thumbs-up and Claudia, who had crawled into her closet to look for snacks, called over her shoulder, "Sign me up."

Mary Anne nodded and printed their names into the calendar in her neat, precise handwriting.

Mary Anne, as I mentioned earlier, is Kristy's best friend, which proves that opposites really do attract. While Kristy can sometimes be a real big-mouth, Mary Anne Spier ranks as one of the shyest people on the planet. She is a little taller than Kristy, with a very cool short haircut and big brown eyes that fill with tears at the drop of a hat. I'm not kidding. Mary Anne will even cry at TV commercials — especially ones that involve any kind of baby animal (though kittens, like her own, Tigger, are her favorites).

Whereas Kristy is a talker, Mary Anne is a great listener. She's sensitive and honest and a true-blue friend.

You'd think that, being such a shy person, Mary Anne wouldn't have a boyfriend. But she does. In fact, Mary Anne was the first one in the BSC to have a steady guy.

Logan Bruno is her boyfriend's name. He's very cute and has this charming Southern accent. But the best thing about him is he likes to baby-sit. In fact, he's one of our associate members. Isn't that cool?

Mary Anne's life has been as complicated as Kristy's. Maybe even more so. You see, Mary Anne's mom died when Mary Anne was a baby. So Mr. Spier had to raise her all by himself. He was a good dad but a little on the overprotective side. He used to make Mary Anne dress in babyish clothes. And Mary Anne was only allowed to talk on the phone if it was about schoolwork.

Those things began to change, though, around the time Mary Anne's father met Sharon Schafer. Or I guess I should say, remet.

15

How did it happen? Well, Sharon grew up in Stoneybrook, but went to California for college and, as it turned out, stayed and married there. When her marriage ended, she moved back to town with her two kids, Dawn and Jeff. Dawn and Mary Anne met and became instant best friends. Kristy was jealous at first but soon accepted the fact that Mary Anne could have two best friends.

Here's the strange part of the story: One night, Dawn and Mary Anne were looking through Sharon's old Stoneybrook High School yearbook. That's when they discovered that Mary Anne's dad, Richard, and Sharon had been high school sweethearts.

Ding! A little bell went off in their heads. Why not get their parents back together? And that's what they did.

Soon Richard and Sharon were dating, and before they knew it they were married. Mary Anne and Richard moved into Sharon's and Dawn's old farmhouse on Burnt Hill Road, and Mary Anne and Dawn went from being best friends to stepsisters. It was a dream come true.

Dawn started to miss her dad and her brother, Jeff, who had already moved back to the West Coast. And as much as she loved living with Mary Anne, Dawn felt her heart was in California. Finally Dawn moved back there, but we've kept her on as our honorary member, and we stay in touch with letters and through Mary Anne's phone calls to Dawn.

One more thing about Mary Anne. She's our club secretary. That means she's in charge of the BSC record book. It's an extremely important book. Along with the calendar of sitting jobs, it contains the names and addresses of our clients and other essential information.

Mary Anne assigns our jobs. She has to know, in advance, every BSC member's conflicts: doctor appointments, after-school activities, music and dance lessons, you name it. I told you I was organized, but Mary Anne is super-organized. And you know what? She has never, *ever* made a mistake.

Our treasurer is Stacey McGill. She's a math whiz. On Mondays, she collects our dues. She keeps the cash in a manila envelope. The money buys supplies for projects, pays for Claudia's phone bill (she has her own phone line), and contributes to Charlie Thomas's gas money (he drives Kristy and Abby to our meetings).

Stacey was born and raised in New York City, and it shows. She is sophisticated, cool, gorgeous, smart — did I mention gorgeous? You don't need to read a fashion magazine to find out the latest fashion trend. Just check out Stacey.

But life isn't perfect for Stacey McGill. Far

from it. Her parents are divorced, and she had to make a tough decision — whether to live with her mom in Stoneybrook or her dad in New York. After weighing the options, she picked Stoneybrook.

Another thing that isn't perfect about Stacey is her health. She's diabetic, which means her body has trouble regulating the amount of sugar in her bloodstream. She has to watch her diet very, very carefully and give herself injections of insulin every single day. She's a real trouper about it, and you hardly ever hear her complain.

Stacey's best friend is Claudia Kishi, another gorgeous, cool, talented person. Claudia is Japanese-American and has straight, black, shiny hair that is to die for, as well as a beautiful, spotless complexion. Which is pretty amazing considering what she eats. Claud is the junk food queen. Mallomars, chocolate stars, cheese puffs — you name it, Claudia probably has it stashed somewhere in her room.

Today she offered around a bag of pretzels, plus Cheez Whiz that had magically appeared from a shoe box at the back of her closet.

Claudia is an artist and sees the whole world as her palette. She tie-dyes her T-shirts, makes her own earrings, and puts together one-of-a-kind outfits. On that day she was wearing denim overall shorts, a short black T-shirt, red-

and-white pin-striped stockings that came over the tops of her knees, red thick-soled patent leather shoes, and a black felt derby.

Claudia would rather create artwork than do anything else, and that used to show on her report card. Of course, that was when Claudia was struggling to keep up with her eighth-grade classes. Then her parents and teachers decided Claudia should be put back in seventh grade. It was a tough decision for everyone, but they felt she would be better off. And you know what? They were right. Her grades have really improved, so Claudia is happy.

Claudia is our vice-president, mainly because our meetings are held at her house and she is the only one of us to have her own phone in her room.

Abigail Stevenson is our alternate officer. That means she takes over the duties of any regular officer who's absent. Abby's dad died four years ago (in a car accident, but she doesn't like to talk about that). After Mr. Stevenson died, Abby's mom took a job at a publishing company in Manhattan and commuted from their house on Long Island to the city. But not long ago, she was promoted and was able to buy a bigger house. And the house she found was in Stoneybrook, right down the street from Kristy.

How would I describe Abby? Big! Not in

body, but in personality. She's outgoing and hilarious, and she talks fast, in a very loud voice. She explains it by saying, "I'm from Long Island. You have to talk fast to get a word in edgewise."

Abby is allergic to just about everything and suffers from asthma, but she doesn't let that stop her from doing anything. In fact, Abby hikes, runs, skis and plays tennis, soccer, and softball. Talk about a major athlete.

You want to know one more thing about Abby? She is an identical twin. Yes, there is another thirteen-year-old eighth-grader with thick black hair that falls into ringlets, super-dark brown eyes, and sharp, pretty features walking around the streets of Stoneybrook. Her name is Anna.

But Abby and Anna are easy to tell apart. Anna's hair is shorter, for one thing. The girls dress differently, too. Abby, the athlete, can usually be found in bike shorts and a T-shirt, whereas Anna, the musician, would more likely wear a dress. And when it comes to personalities, they're practically opposites.

Anna is shy and private. She plays violin in the SMS orchestra, and practices all the time. When we invited Abby to join our club, we asked Anna, too, but she declined. Her music keeps her too busy.

I've already told you that Jessi and I are the

BSC's junior officers. We're the youngest (everyone else is thirteen), and we aren't allowed to baby-sit as late as the other members. We take a lot of the after-school and weekend jobs.

That covers everybody except the associate members. Logan Bruno, as I mentioned, is one, and Shannon Kilbourne is the other. Shannon goes to Stoneybrook Day School where she's in a million clubs and is an honor student. She's incredibly busy, so it's a good thing she and Logan are not required to attend meetings or pay dues. They just fill in when we're extra busy.

Now back to the meeting.

Rrrrring!

The phone was ringing again. (I told you, some days it rings nonstop.)

"I'll answer it," I called, reaching for the receiver. "Baby-sitters Club. This is Mallory."

"Mal?" a young voice said. "This is Buddy Barrett."

"Buddy!" I repeated in surprise. Most of our calls are from adults. We rarely hear from one of our charges during a meeting. Since Kristy had just spoken to Buddy's mom, Mrs. DeWitt, this seemed especially odd.

"What's up?" I asked.

"I'm in trouble!" Buddy replied. His voice quivered a little. "Lindsey told me she was going to be in the parade. I told her I wanted to be in it, too. But they said I couldn't — "

"Now, hold on," I interrupted. "Are you talking about the Memorial Day parade?"

"Yes!" Buddy replied. "Lindsey's Brownie troop is going to march in it."

Lindsey DeWitt is Buddy's stepsister. She's eight, and so is Buddy.

"But why are you in trouble?" I asked Buddy.

"Because they said I couldn't march in the parade unless I belonged to a group." There was a long pause. Finally Buddy said in a tiny voice, "So I made one up."

"You made up a group?" I repeated. "What kind of group?"

"I told them I was in a marching band," Buddy said miserably. "Now what do I do? I don't even know how to play an instrument."

"Okay, don't panic," I said in my calmest voice. "There should be some way we can solve this. Let me talk to the others and I'll call you right back."

"Thanks, Mal," Buddy said. "You're the best."

Six pairs of eyes were staring at me when I hung up the phone.

Abby spoke first. "Well? Tell us what's going on. The suspense is killing me."

I explained Buddy's problem.

"That makes me so mad!" Kristy replied. "The Boy and Girl Scouts, including the Cub Scouts and Brownies, always march in the parade. But what about all of those other kids who don't belong to any groups? They should be able to be in the parade, too."

I started to feel that tingle on the back of my neck. The one that lets me know Kristy is about to come up with another one of her Great Ideas.

"Buddy told them he had a marching band?" Now Kristy was standing. "Then we'll give him a marching band!"

"But who will be in the band with Buddy?" Mary Anne asked logically.

"Lots of kids," Kristy answered. "How about the members of All the Children of the World?"

All the Children of the World is the name of a musical group a bunch of our charges once formed. They played instruments and sang songs from the musical *Fiddler on the Roof* in a performance at the Newtons' house.

"But they're not exactly a band," Stacey pointed out. "Only a few of them really play instruments."

"Minor detail!" Kristy replied with a wave of her hand. She was now pacing back and forth across Claudia's room. "We'll work that out. We've faced tougher problems than this."

Mary Anne, who was sitting cross-legged on

the bed with the record book in her lap, flipped to the calendar again. "Well, the parade is a little over three weeks away."

Stacey winced. "Can we organize all of those children in three weeks?"

"Three weeks?" Kristy looked up abruptly.

Mary Anne nodded. "And a couple of days."

A confident grin spread across Kristy's face. "That's plenty of time."

Kristy is amazing. During the last ten minutes of our meeting, she managed to convince us that if we put on our thinking caps, we'd be able to organize a big band of children, teach them to play instruments, and even make their costumes — all in less than twenty-five days!

CHAPTER 3

"Salutations!" called out Mr. Cobb on Monday morning.

Our Short Takes teacher stood at the front of the classroom. He was dressed in a collarless white shirt, jeans, and a black vest. His sun-streaked hair looked great with his deep tan and gleaming white teeth. Was he cool? Totally. Did I luck out being picked for his class? You bet.

"Can anyone tell me what book that's from?" Mr. Cobb asked, surveying the room with his clear blue eyes. His gaze settled on Jimmy Bouloukos in the front row.

"Jimmy? Do you know the answer?" Mr. Cobb tapped on his desk.

"It's on the tip of my tongue," Jimmy replied. "Give me a second."

In the meantime, Megan Armstrong, a Korean girl who was new to our school, raised her

25

hand. "Isn't that what Charlotte the spider says to Wilbur in *Charlotte's Web*?"

Mr. Cobb touched the tip of his tanned nose. "Exactomundo."

He perched on the edge of his desk and crossed his arms. "*Charlotte's Web*, by E. B. White, is one of the great classics of children's literature. We won't be studying that book in this course, but it's good that you know the field."

I smiled to myself. When it comes to children's books, I definitely know the field. Not only do I spend most nights reading my brothers and sisters to sleep, but plenty of my free time is filled devouring all the great children's books I can find.

"I'm pretty new to Stoneybrook, so let me start by telling you a little bit about myself," Mr. Cobb said, flashing his teeth at the class again. "I graduated from Princeton with a master's degree in American literature. But I grew up in Florida. I love books, obviously, but I'm also a sports fanatic."

"All right, Coach Cobb!" Glen Johnson called from across the room.

"If you don't know it already, I'm assistant coach of the baseball team," Mr. Cobb added, flipping his blond hair off his forehead. "I volunteered to teach this course because analyzing literature for all ages may rank up there as my favorite thing." He hopped off the edge of the desk. "And that's what we're going to do. For the next few weeks, we'll be engaged in an in-depth analysis of what makes a good read for young kids."

This was going to be great. I patted my notebook as he strolled down the aisle. Over the weekend, I'd bought a brand-new, forest green ringbinder especially for this class. My pencils were sharpened, and I'd even stocked up on two new pens. I was ready to work.

Mr. Cobb paused by my desk and stared down at my notebook. Everyone in the room had turned in their seats, and they were looking at us. Mr. Cobb pointed to my notebook. "Put that away," he said.

I blinked up at him. "Put what away?" I asked.

"That notebook." He waved his hand over my supplies. "Those pens, that paper. You won't need them."

I could feel my cheeks start to heat up. I tucked a strand of hair behind one ear and said, "But I don't understand. I thought we would be writing a lot of papers."

"Wrong!" He spun dramatically. "We will be doing a lot of thinking. This course is a meeting of the minds."

Mr. Cobb walked down the aisle pointing at papers and notebooks on kids' desks. "Put away your writing materials. Put everything away. There will be no tests or papers."

"Cool!" Benny Ott said, tossing his notebook over his shoulder.

"Every day our class will meet in this room and talk," Mr. Cobb explained. "I'm hoping for a very active and stimulating exchange of ideas."

"My kind of class," Liz Cohen declared.

A lot of kids were happy about not having to take tests or write any stories or essays. But not me. I love to write. I think better with a pen in my hand.

"But Mr. Cobb, how will you grade us?" asked Elise Coates.

Our teacher leaned against his desk again, a confident smile on his face. "By your participation. By how well you express your thoughts and ideas with the rest of us. So be prepared to speak up."

My stomach sank. This was starting to sound more like a debate class than a literature class.

Mr. Cobb waved his hands like a wizard casting a spell. "Clear your desks," he announced, "and we'll begin."

I hurriedly tucked my notebook under my chair. No way was I going to have him make an example of me again.

"The first author-illustrator we will be discussing is Maurice Sendak."

That was the best news I'd heard all day. I love Maurice Sendak. His book *Where the Wild Things Are* has always been a Pike family favorite.

"We will also be doing on-the-spot analyses of books in the class," he continued. "Reading and commenting on them as we go."

"Hey, Coach!" Chris Brooks called.

"Yes, Chris?" Mr. Cobb gave him a warm smile. Chris was on the baseball team with Mr. Cobb.

"Do you want us to bring in the books?" Chris asked. "Or will you supply them?"

Mr. Cobb jabbed the air with his finger. "*Good* question. I'll bring the books for the first couple of weeks and then I'll ask you to bring in your favorites."

My heart started to thud a little faster. My favorites? I had so many of them. It would be hard to pick just one. What if Mr. Cobb or the rest of the class thought my choice was stupid?

I tried to push that thought out of my head.

Megan Armstrong raised her hand. "So there won't be any written work at all?"

Mr. Cobb squeezed one eye shut. "Well, actually . . . you caught me. There will be *one* paper."

Several students groaned and Mr. Cobb burst out laughing. "I want you all to write an essay on a subject of your choosing."

"*Any* subject?" Chris called. "Like the merits of using a wooden bat versus an aluminum bat in softball?"

"You wish," Mr. Cobb said, rapping his knuckles on Chris's desk. "No, this paper will be about an end-of-the-class project that will further the cause of children's literature." He pointed at Jimmy Bouloukos's head. "Put that in the hopper and think about it."

It's funny. As I watched Mr. Cobb joke casually with some of the students he already knew, an uneasy feeling started to bubble inside me. I felt like a newcomer. Not just to this class or school, but to the subject of children's literature.

When the bell rang, Sandra Hart, our sixth grade vice-president, sidled up beside me. "Ooh, Mr. Cobb is so cute," she whispered. "How old do you think he is?"

"I don't know," I replied with a backward glance at our teacher. "Older than us."

Sandra poked my arm lightly. "Oh, come on. Don't tell me you don't care!"

I stared down at my notebook, which I was clutching to my chest. "Well, actually, I was thinking about something else," I confessed. "I'm a little worried about how the class participation is going to work."

Sandra tossed her long hair over one shoulder. "I think it's great. No papers."

"But I don't mind papers," I said.

Sandra rolled her eyes. "That's because you're a brain."

I opened my mouth to protest, but Sandra cut me off. "I heard all about your straight A's. Why should you worry about anything?"

I shut my mouth. How could I explain to Sandra that the grades didn't matter (though I certainly didn't mind them)? It was doing my best work that counted.

That night I reread every Maurice Sendak book we had in the house. I knew we weren't supposed to write anything down, but I couldn't help it. I made notes about the stories, particularly the unusual plot turns. I even noted when each book was written, in case that came up in the class discussion.

I'd been at it for an hour when I heard a soft knocking on the door.

Tap, tap, tap.

It was Vanessa. "Sorry to interrupt you when you're working," she said. "But you have a phone call. It's Jessi."

I'd just seen Jessi at the BSC meeting that afternoon, but I guessed a quick break wouldn't hurt things.

"Hi, Jessi," I said into the phone. "What's up?"

"I just talked to Claudia, who just talked to Stacey, who just talked to Kristy," she said in one long breath. "And . . ."

"And what?"

"After the meeting today, Kristy had another one of her great ideas. And she decided that the BSC should help Buddy and the kids make the instruments for their marching band."

"Wow, things move fast around here," I said with a low whistle. "I mean, we were only thinking about talking a few of the kids into joining Buddy."

Jessi chuckled. "Now we have a full-fledged band. All we need to do is make the instruments."

"But how, and when, are we going to make these instruments?" I asked.

"Kristy has that all figured out," Jessi explained. "Claudia is gathering the supplies. We can pick them up at her house. Kristy suggested we all work on the instruments when we're on our next sitting jobs."

I nodded, even though I was on the phone. "Good idea — as usual."

"All we have to do is make drums and stringed instruments," Jessi continued.

"*All?*" I repeated. "I hope the supplies Claudia's giving us come with instructions."

Jessi giggled. "Me, too."

I checked my watch. I'd been talking for five minutes. Break time was over. I wanted to finish my homework. I said good-bye to Jessi and hurried back to my room. But instead of my homework, I found two little girls with big blue eyes sitting on my bed.

"Mal, it's story time," Claire announced with an ear-to-ear grin.

Margo scooted sideways to make room for me and patted my pillow. "You promised."

I looked wistfully at my stack of books and the open notebook sitting on my desk. My homework could wait. After all, a promise is a promise.

But just to kill two birds with one stone, as they say, I grabbed a Maurice Sendak book and settled in between my two sisters.

I opened the cover, and the girls giggled as they looked at the little boy in the white costume with the pointy ears and big feet.

I pointed to the words and read the first line. " 'The night Max wore his wolf suit and made mischief of one kind and another . . .' "

"You're a good reader," Claire said, looking at me with adoring eyes.

Margo squeezed my arm. "The best!"

That night, visions of Max and his wild things danced through my dreams. The images were still vivid when I walked into Mr. Cobb's class the next day.

The bell had barely finished ringing before Mr. Cobb asked the first question.

"The title of Maurice Sendak's book is *Where the Wild Things Are*," he said, facing our group. "So where exactly *are* the wild things?"

I was the first to raise my hand. Behind me I heard someone whisper, "Miss Know-it-all," and I quickly lowered my hand. But then I remembered Mr. Cobb's plan to grade on participation, so I shoved my hand in the air again.

Mr. Cobb smiled vaguely at me, then scanned the room as several more hands shot up. He pointed to Randy Rademacher. "Yes, Randy. Where are Sendak's wild things?"

"Well, Sendak says they are a day and a night away. So I'd say they're on the other side of Max's world."

"The other side, huh?" Mr. Cobb scratched his chin.

"Yeah, like a good and a bad world," Craig Avazian piped up. "In the good world, he's a regular kid. But in the bad, he's a wild king."

I frowned. I didn't agree with Craig or Randy at all. I thought the wild things were in Max's imagination.

My arm was still up, and it was starting to tingle. I was about to switch arms, but something made me hesitate. Mr. Cobb seemed so enthusiastic about what Randy and Craig were saying that I started to think maybe my idea was wrong. I lowered my arm.

"This is great," Mr. Cobb said, rubbing his hands together. "Now on to the next question. Why doesn't Max stay in the Land of the Wild Things?"

I raised my hand again. So did Jen Corn and Megan Armstrong.

"I think Max decided he couldn't be all bad," Jimmy Bouloukos called out without raising his hand. "There has to be a balance. So Max decided to come back to the good world and be a good kid for awhile."

I had a very different opinion. This time, I switched arms. But Robbie Mara and Benny Ott started talking about the wild rumpus dance, and the subject was changed before I could be called on.

Chris Brooks and Liz Cohen had a heated discussion about dreams versus reality. I really would have liked to be in on that, but Mr. Cobb didn't seem to notice me.

About halfway through the class, Mr. Cobb said, "What do you say we all take a five-minute break? Stand up. Stretch. Have a drink of water, whatever."

I looked at the classroom clock. A lot of time had passed and I hadn't said a word. I'd raised my hand at least ten times, but Mr. Cobb hadn't called on me once.

At the water fountain, Sandra Hart whispered to me, "Isn't Craig Avazian a major babe? Did you hear what he said about the rumpus dance being a jungle rite? Totally cool."

I swallowed the water and wiped my mouth with the back of my hand. "Yeah, but I really think that this whole story takes place in Max's imagination. Maybe it's even a dream."

Sandra took a sip of water and looked at me sideways but didn't say anything.

After the break, Mr. Cobb walked to the portable bookshelf in front of the board and withdrew a book. "It's now time for us to read and discuss. This is the on-the-spot analysis portion of our class."

My insides tightened. I wasn't sure I could analyze something just like that. What if my opinion was wrong?

Mr. Cobb held the book in one hand and looked out at the class. I watched him pause at my row. I slumped down in my seat, trying to blend in with the other students.

"You there," he said, pointing right at me. "You in the third row. What's your name?"

I pointed to myself and croaked. "Me?"

Several of the kids giggled.

"Yes, you. What's your name?"

"Just call her the Brain," Benny muttered from behind me.

I cleared my throat. "Mallory. Mallory Pike," I said in a tiny voice.

Mr. Cobb cupped his hand around one ear. "Valerie?"

Now there was snickering all around me.

I was about to correct him when he stuck the book in front of my face and said, "Why don't you read us this book, Valerie?"

I looked at the book and read the title in a shaky voice. *"Green Eggs and Ham."*

"Louder!" Megan called from her place in the front row.

I took that to mean faster. My words tumbled out in a tangled rush.

I'm usually a good speaker, with a loud, clear voice. But not that day. I could barely read, let alone talk.

" 'I do not like them in a house,' " I continued reading. " 'I do not like them here or there.' "

Mr. Cobb, who had been standing behind me, cleared his throat and interrupted, "Valerie, you skipped 'I do not like them with a mouse.' "

I stared down at the page, confused. How could that happen?

I reread the page, this time very slowly, to make sure I didn't miss any words. Behind me I could hear Benny Ott making snoring sounds, as if I were putting him to sleep.

My ears, my cheeks, my freckles — my entire body was flaming beet red. I could hear a rushing sound in my ears.

While my mouth was reading the words, my brain was screaming, "Please, take the book from me. Give it to someone else!"

Rrrrring!

I froze in midsentence. Was that really the bell or had I just imagined it?

All around me kids were standing up. Mr. Cobb was walking to the front of the room.

The bell had rung. Hooray!

I bolted from my seat and charged for the door. I should have returned the Seuss book to Mr. Cobb. But I left it on my desk. I knew if I spent one more second in that classroom, I'd scream.

Once out of the room, I raced to the girls' bathroom and splashed water on my face. How could so many things go wrong in one class?

First, Mr. Cobb hadn't even noticed me. Then when he did, he got my name wrong, which was humiliating. The kids had teased me about my good grades. But when I was asked to read out loud to the class, something I've always been good at, I choked.

I raised my head and looked in the mirror above the bathroom sink. "*Valerie* Pike," I murmured to my reflection. "It fits. Valerie, the-totally-mixed-up Pike."

CHAPTER 4

Wednesday-Music Mutilation night
Hey, Claud, here's a riddle for you:
What do you get when you take 7 kids,
add 3 boxes of Kleenex, 4 toilet-paper
tubes, 2 oatmeal boxes, and 3 balls
of string?

I dont know, Stacey, waht do you git?

Well, you sure don't get an orchestra.
But you do get one wild night at the
Barrett-DeWitts...

Stacey wasn't exaggerating. About the music. Or the wild night. Of course, every night at the Barrett-DeWitts' is pretty crazy. They're a big, blended family. You see, Mrs. Barrett had three children — Buddy, who's eight, five-year-old Suzi, and two-year-old Marnie. When she married Franklin DeWitt not long ago, the family more than doubled in size, because he had *four* children: Lindsey, who's eight; Taylor, six; Madeleine, four; and Ryan, two.

This was the first evening that Kristy's plan, to baby-sit for kids and build musical instruments at the same time, was to go into effect.

Claudia had loaded a red wagon with cardboard boxes of all shapes and sizes, while Stacey had brought several items from her recycling bin — old plastic bottles, toilet-paper and paper-towel tubes, and newspapers.

Stacey was dressed in a "Let's build something" outfit — jeans with rolled-up cuffs, an oversized blue denim work shirt, and a painter's cap turned backward.

Claudia wore shorts and a rainbow tie-dyed T-shirt. Her hair was pulled into a thick ponytail held by a matching tie-dyed scrunchie. Since this was to be a work party, she sported her favorite work shoes, red high-top sneakers.

When Stacey and Claudia rolled up to the

front door of the Barrett-DeWitt house, Madeleine met them at the door. "Wook evwe boddee," she mumbled through a mouthful of peanut butter and jelly. "It's a pawade."

Stacey whispered to Claudia, "Translation — 'Look, everybody, it's a parade.' "

Claudia waved to Madeleine. "You ain't seen nothing yet! What we have here is a wagon full of gen-u-ine magical music makers."

Madeleine raced back inside, shouting, "Hey, there's magic! Stacey and Claud brought magic!"

Word spread fast about the magical music makers.

Stacey and Claudia grinned at each other as they listened to the sound of feet pounding toward them from every direction in the house.

Buddy was the first to appear. He spotted the supplies in Claudia's wagon and his face lit up. "All right!" he cried. "You brought the instruments!"

Stacey stared down at the pile of cardboard boxes and plastic jugs. "That's some imagination!"

"Come on in!" Buddy grabbed the wagon and tugged it over the threshold into the living room.

Mr. and Mrs. DeWitt were just coming down the stairs. Madeleine, Marnie, and Ryan were jumping all around them like excited puppies.

"A parade!" Madeleine cried. "We're going to be in a parade!"

Mrs. DeWitt looked up at Stacey and Claud in surprise. "Is this true? Are all the kids going to be in the Memorial Day parade?"

Claudia nodded at Buddy. "It was Buddy's idea. He thought the kids should form a marching band."

"You thought of this?" Mrs. DeWitt asked Buddy.

Buddy blushed and dug the toe of his sneaker into the carpet. "Uh, I guess so."

"You see, Buddy doesn't think it's fair that only organized groups like the Scouts are allowed to march," Claudia explained. "He thinks any kid should be able to participate — "

"And so do we," Stacey put in. "So we're turning your house into a musical-instrument workshop."

Mr. DeWitt looked alarmed. "You mean, with saws and drills?"

"No," Claudia giggled. She gestured to the wagon full of supplies. "This workshop will only use tape, glue, and blunt scissors."

Stacey and Claudia watched Mr. DeWitt relax. "Well, I know the kids are in good hands," he said with a relieved grin.

As they were leaving, Mrs. DeWitt whispered, "Try not to make too big a mess. We finally managed to clean the house today."

Claudia whispered back, "We'll be the clean machine."

Two minutes after the front door closed, the house looked like a bomb had exploded. Cardboard, string, and tape were strewn everywhere. And everyone was shouting.

Taylor ran for the wagon and grabbed a round oatmeal box. "I want to make a drum," he shouted.

Buddy rifled through the boxes until he found the other round oatmeal box. "Me, too!" he yelled.

"Me, too! Me, too!" Ryan cried, trying to pull the box out of Taylor's hands.

"Here." Stacey reached for the nearest item — a toilet-paper tube — and shoved it into Ryan's hand. "You can make a trumpet."

But Marnie wanted the toilet-paper tube. "Me first!" she shouted. "Give it to me!"

While Stacey hunted for another tube, Claudia tried to show Buddy and Taylor how to make a drum.

In the meantime, Suzi Barrett was carefully picking over the rest of the supplies. She grabbed some string, three or four boxes, and a long paper-towel tube and carried it all to the far corner of the room.

"Hey!" Madeleine cried, folding her arms

across her chest. "Suzi took all of the best stuff."

"Did not!" Suzi shot back.

"Did, too!"

Claudia left the boys with the drums and raced to do damage control with the girls. "There are still plenty of supplies left, Madeleine. Look, here's a fun jug." Claud held up a plastic milk jug. "You can blow in it and make noise."

Madeleine wasn't happy. "That's just a stupid old milk jug."

"Not if you decorate it." Claudia held up some felt strips and a glue stick.

Madeleine reluctantly accepted the felt and glue. And for one second a truce was declared. Then Lindsey came into the living room.

She walked to the wagon and carefully chose a tissue box, a paper-towel tube, a handful of rubber bands, and some tape.

Buddy looked up from where he was working at the coffee table. "Wait a minute. What are you doing?" he demanded.

"I'm making a guitar," Lindsey replied.

Buddy jumped up and grabbed the tissue box. "Oh, no you don't. You're not in this band."

"She can be in the band if she wants to be," Taylor cried, leaping to Lindsey's defense.

"No way!" Buddy shouted. "Lindsey's going to march with the Brownies. She can't do both."

Stacey covered her ears with her hands and cried, "Stop it! Both of you. Stop shouting."

The room went silent.

Stacey lowered her hands and spoke in a calm voice. "There. That's better. Now, this was supposed to be a fun evening, but we seem to be totally off course."

"I'll say." Claudia gestured to the living room littered with art supplies and pieces of cardboard. "It looks like we've been hit by a tornado. Remember what your mother said? Don't mess up the house."

Stacey suddenly held up one hand. "Wait a minute. Did you hear that?"

The children froze.

"Hear what?" Buddy whispered.

"That sound." Stacey tiptoed to the front window and peered out through the curtain. "I thought I heard a car. What if it's your parents? And they've forgotten something."

The children stared at Stacey with big, unblinking eyes.

"Oh, no," Madeleine gasped.

Claudia whispered, "What will they say when they see this mess?"

Suzi spoke first. "They'll say we're in big trouble."

Claudia nodded solemnly. "That's right. So what should we do about it?"

The kids cried, "Clean up!"

"Good idea!" Claudia replied. "I'll help you guys pick this mess up — " She looked over at Stacey, who was still pretending to look though the curtain. "Stacey?"

"Yes?" Stacey whispered dramatically.

Claudia winked at her. "You stand guard."

"Right!"

Minutes later, the supplies had been picked up and put away. The children were gathered around either the coffee table in the living room or the dining table, happily building their instruments.

Buddy finished his instrument first and held it up for everyone to see. He'd taped paper to the top of the oatmeal box and glued star stickers around the sides. "Here's my drum. Listen." He thumped on it a few times.

"Way to go," Stacey declared.

"Here's my guitar!" Lindsey held up her tissue box with rubber bands stretched across the hole. "If there's a kid in your band who doesn't have an instrument," she told Buddy, "he can use mine."

Buddy gave her a thumbs-up.

"Thanks, Lindsey," Claudia said. "That was really thoughtful."

Suzi looked up at Stacey with a quivering chin. "Something's wrong with mine." She'd taped two toilet-paper tubes to the side of a box and tried to wrap string around them. "I don't even know what it is."

Stacey held the weird contraption in the air, twisting it right, then left. Finally she announced, "Look, everybody, Suzi has invented a new instrument!"

"What's it called?" Taylor asked.

"It's a . . ." Stacey squeezed one eye closed, trying to think quickly. "A google-blaster."

"A google-blaster!" Taylor clutched his sides and rolled on the rug, laughing.

"Look!" Stacey hummed into both tubes. "And it really plays!"

"Stacey!" Marnie cried. "What mine?"

Stacey circled the table to look at Marnie's invention — a milk jug plastered with tangled-up tape. "This is most definitely a snorka-phone."

"I want to make a snorkaphone!" Madeleine squealed with delight. In seconds she'd wadded up tape and stickers and attached them to her milk jug.

Taylor dove for the tape and circled his entire drum with toilet-paper tubes. When he was finished, he leaped to his feet and yelled, "Ta-dah!"

Claudia clapped her hands together. "It looks great, Taylor. What are you going to call it?"

Taylor scratched his chin, staring at his instrument. Finally he raised his head and declared, "This is a hum-drum. See? You can hum into the tubes and drum on the box."

"Brilliant!" Claud gave him a high five.

All the kids were chattering at once, vying to see who could make up the silliest name.

In the midst of the giggling, a tiny bell trilled.

Stacey cocked her head and held up one hand. "Do you hear something? What kind of instrument is that?"

"Sounds like a jingle-hopper," Buddy joked.

"Or a . . ." Stacey's eyes grew huge, as she realized what the sound really was. "Phone! We better answer it. Quick. Your parents could be calling."

Several kids dove for the phone in the kitchen, but it was Lindsey who answered it. "This is the Barrett-DeWitts'."

Lindsey paused for several seconds and then turned to Claudia. "It's Mary Anne. She wants to talk to you." She covered the receiver and whispered, "She sounds upset."

"Hey, Mary Anne," Claudia said as she took the phone. "What's up?"

"I'm over here with Jenny Prezzioso," Mary Anne explained, "and we've just spent an entire hour trying to make a musical instrument."

"And?"

"Well, all we've come up with is this boxy-looking thing with tubes attached to the sides and a lot of tape."

"Oh." Claudia giggled. "Sounds like you've made a google-blaster."

There was a long pause. Finally Mary Anne said, "A what?"

"A google-blaster." Claudia explained, "We have several instruments over here that look just like that."

Mary Anne sighed with relief. "I was afraid you guys were making artsy trumpets and drums."

"Are you kidding?" Claudia gasped. "We stopped trying to do that hours ago. Now we have our own unique band."

"But do the instruments play?"

Now it was Claud's turn to pause. "I'm not sure. Let me see." Claudia looked over at Stacey. "Mary Anne wants to know if we can actually play our instruments."

Stacey shrugged. "I don't know. Why don't we find out?"

Stacey told the Barretts and DeWitts to line up together with their snorkaphones, google-blasters, and hum-drums while Claudia held the phone out for Mary Anne to hear.

Stacey raised her hands in front of her like a conductor. "On the count of three, we'll play 'Jingle Bells.' A-one, and a-two, and a — "

Moo! Honk! Thud!

No matter what the kids did, only thumps and hollow groaning sounds came out of their instruments.

Claudia slowly brought the phone back to her ear. "Did you hear that?" she asked.

"I sure did," Mary Anne replied. "What *was* that? It sounded terrible."

Claudia tried to answer in a cheery voice. "That was our band."

"Oh, no." Mary Anne groaned.

"You can say that again," Claudia replied.

A little while later, the DeWitt and Barrett kids put down their instruments and started their bedtime snack of apple slices and yogurt in the kitchen. That's when Stacey gestured for Claudia to join her in the living room.

"I hate to break it to Kristy and the others," Stacey whispered to Claudia, "but I think this parade is going to be a *disaster.*"

CHAPTER 5

"This meeting of the sixth-grade officers is called to order," Justin Price declared.

It was Thursday morning, just before school. I'd talked to the other officers, and we'd agreed to meet before class in the Memory Garden.

I love that place. It's a beautiful little garden with a bench and a plaque in memory of an eighth-grader, Amelia Freeman, who was killed by a drunk driver. Mary Anne was so moved by the loss of Amelia that she thought of creating the garden as a memorial. Amelia's death affected all of us and even spurred the creation of SMS's chapter of S.A.D.D. (Students Against Drunk Driving).

Justin was sitting on the bench next to Sandra Hart. He focused his dark brown eyes on me and said, "Mallory, why don't you give us an update on the sixth-grade fund-raiser?"

"Okay." I sat cross-legged on the grass beside Lisa Mannheim, our class treasurer. I opened my notebook labeled "FUN-raiser" and began my report.

"The fund-raiser is at this moment less than fourteen days away. Last year the sixth grade ran a candy store for the entire week, but kids stopped buying toward the end. So my committee and I decided to set up five different booths, one for each day of the week."

"Good idea," Sandra said after Justin had nodded his approval. "This way kids won't get bored."

"We're declaring the entire week a FUN-raiser."

Lisa laughed. "That's really clever, Mal. Have you decided what each booth will sell?"

I flipped to the next page in my notebook and read out loud, "Monday, hearts and flowers. Tuesday, T-shirt painting. Wednesday, slam-dunk the teachers. Thursday, candy. We have to sell it one day. And Friday . . ." I looked up and wiggled my eyebrows. "Friday is a secret."

"A secret?" Sandra repeated. "Ooh, I like that."

"Well, Mal," Justin said, rubbing his hands together, "it sounds like you have everything under control. Good work."

I grinned, feeling a little color creep into my cheeks. It's always nice to hear a compliment, but it's extra special when it comes from our class president.

Lisa's precise voice broke into my thoughts. "It sounds as if Mallory has the booths all organized, but we still have one small problem."

Justin cocked his head. "What's that?"

"We haven't decided what we will do with the money," Lisa explained. "That is a very important decision."

Justin adjusted the cap he was wearing. "Right. That's why we're meeting. Whatever we choose to fund will be our class's legacy to the school."

I nodded. "Kids will remember our class for what we gave to SMS."

Lisa pushed her glasses up on her nose. "We need to choose carefully."

"It should be something really cool." Justin squinted off in the distance. "What about buying new sports equipment for the gym?"

I hate gym, but I wrote Justin's suggestion down, since I am the secretary.

"Kids have been complaining about the tumbling mats being worn out, and there are never enough basketballs," he continued.

I don't like to disagree with Justin but I really didn't want my class to donate sports equipment. Let next year's class do that.

"Not everyone's a sports fan," I pointed out

as diplomatically as possible. "Maybe we should think of something that would benefit everybody."

Lisa tapped her pen on her notepad. "What about the school lockers? They could really use a paint job. Mine is peeling and has graffiti all over it."

"We *could* paint the lockers," Justin agreed. "But they'd just need another paint job in a few years. We need to give the school something that will last."

Sandra wasn't participating in our discussion. First she dug in her purse for a brush, which she then ran through her hair. Then she applied lip gloss. Finally, she focused all her attention on waving to kids (especially the boys) who were coming onto the school grounds.

"Sandra." Lisa leaned forward and tapped her on the knee. "Are you paying attention?"

Sandra blinked several times. Finally she confessed, "Not really."

Justin turned to her. "Don't you care where the money goes?"

Sandra tucked her hair behind one ear and said, "Your ideas sounded just great, Justin. Whatever you decide is fine with me."

I rolled my eyes at Lisa. From the way Sandra was talking, you'd think Justin was the only person who mattered at our meeting.

"Do you guys have any more ideas?" Justin asked Lisa and me.

I looked down at my notebook. Before the meeting, I'd jotted down a few ideas. But something was stopping me from mentioning them.

I glanced over my list. Mirrors for the bathrooms. That sounded stupid. Books for the library — not exciting enough.

If it had been a Baby-sitters Club meeting, I wouldn't have been embarrassed about sharing my ideas. But for some reason I felt intimidated around Justin.

Lisa came up with a few more ideas. Then, just before the bell rang, Justin said, "Mallory, could you take a look at the sixth-grade minutes from past years? I know they store them in the library. We can find out what those classes did, and it might give us a few ideas for our class."

"Sure, Justin," I said, sounding a whole lot like Sandra.

The bell rang. As we headed for our homerooms, Justin called, "Let's meet again tomorrow, okay?"

I didn't see Sandra again until later in the day, when we both raced into Mr. Cobb's class. We were each hurrying for our own reasons. I was hurrying because I didn't want to be late. I was already falling down in the participation department. I didn't want to give Mr. Cobb any other reason to wreck my straight-A average.

Sandra was hurrying because she thought Mr. Cobb was cute.

"I can't wait to see what he's wearing today," she said, giggling, as we opened the door to the class.

Sandra wasn't disappointed. Mr. Cobb looked as handsome as ever. He sported crisp tan chinos, leather boat shoes, and an ice-blue linen shirt that matched the color of his eyes. He defined cute.

"Chris Van Allsburg!" Mr. Cobb announced, holding up a book. "He's my man."

Chris Van Allsburg is one of my top three favorite author-illustrators. It's become a family tradition at the Pike house to read his book *The Polar Express* every Christmas.

You'd think I would have been thrilled at the prospect of discussing Van Allsburg's books. Last week, I might have been. Now, I was afraid that I would say something stupid.

Mr. Cobb leaned back against his desk with his feet crossed at the ankles. "I think I'd have to say *The Mysteries of Harris Burdick* is my favorite book of Allsburg's."

"Mine, too," I blurted out. Just as quickly I covered my mouth.

Mr. Cobb cocked his head. "Valerie? Did you want to say something?"

"It's Mallory," I murmured.

"What?" He cupped his hand around one ear. "You're going to have to speak up."

Megan Armstrong, who was sitting in the front row, said, "She's trying to tell you her name is Mallory, not Valerie."

"Oh. Why didn't you say something before?" Mr. Cobb asked, a perplexed look on his face.

Now everyone was turning around in their seats and staring at me.

Here it comes, I thought, as a burning sensation rushed to my ears, then my cheeks, and then my forehead. I slumped farther and farther down in my seat and stared at my desktop.

"We were discussing Chris Van Allsburg," Mr. Cobb continued. "Was there something you wanted to say about him, Mallory?"

I peeked at Mr. Cobb over the top of my glasses and opened my mouth to speak, but Bobby Gustavson's hand shot up in the air.

"Me! Me! Mr. C.," Bobby shouted.

Mr. Cobb turned away from me. "Bobby, what's on your mind?"

Bobby said, "My family reads *The Polar Express* every Christmas."

I was going to tell Mr. Cobb that. But I

couldn't now. I'd sound like a copycat. I waited until we started talking about *The Wreck of the Zephyr*, Van Allsburg's book about a flying ship, to raise my hand.

I raised my right arm. Then my left. Finally I lay with my head on my left arm, which was holding my right elbow, trying to keep my right hand in the air. But Mr. Cobb didn't call on me for the rest of the class.

Robbie Mara and Jimmy Bouloukos started a heated discussion about one of the books, and several other guys joined in. I do remember Lisa Mannheim being called on once. But mostly, the class was a blur of trying to make Mr. Cobb notice me. By the end, I figured I'd had one chance and blown it. I didn't even try to raise my hand again.

That night, I ate my dinner, then retreated to my room to study. The book Mr. Cobb wanted us to read, *Make Way for Ducklings*, was on my bookshelf. But every time I even looked at it, I started thinking about what a wimp I'd become in Mr. Cobb's class — how I sat with my arm meekly raised, while others shouted out their opinions, and how I finally just gave up trying. It made me feel depressed.

I decided to concentrate on something less upsetting. In my book bag were the sixth-grade minutes from the last ten years at SMS. I settled in to study them.

The first year's notes, from a decade earlier, were handwritten by someone named Christine Schneider. Their fund-raiser had been a bake sale. They'd bought a tree for the courtyard.

"A tree?" I mused out loud. "That's nice. And lasting."

The next two classes had also bought trees or shrubbery. So trees were out.

One class donated chalk. Another donated library books.

I was lying on my bed as I read the records, and I have to admit, my eyelids were getting pretty droopy. Suddenly I spotted something odd.

I blinked several times and rubbed my eyes. Then I sat up.

According to the minutes, five years ago the sixth grade had pledged a thousand dollars to the SMS Library Fund. That money was to go toward purchasing furniture and magazine subscriptions for a student lounge in the library.

"There's no student lounge at my school," I said out loud. "I'm sure there never has been one."

I reread the minutes several times, tracking the class's entire fund-raising efforts. They'd put a lot of time and hard work into raising that thousand dollars.

"So where'd the money go?" I murmured.

Those students were now in high school. I wondered if they knew that their student lounge never happened.

This was definitely a mystery worth looking into. I couldn't wait to tell Justin, Sandra, and Lisa all about it.

CHAPTER 6

"End-of-class projects," Mr. Cobb declared, pointing to the four words he'd written on the blackboard. "Let's take a few moments to discuss your ideas."

It was Friday. The last class of the week. I was sitting in my usual seat, with my usual slump, hoping no one would notice me — as usual.

"What's the theme of the project?" Craig Avazian asked, without raising his hand.

"I would like you to come up with a project that furthers the cause of children's literature," Mr. Cobb replied.

"You mean, like designing a poster campaign using covers from famous books?" Chris Brooks asked.

"Exactomundo," Mr. Cobb said. "That's a great idea."

"Can I steal it?" Robbie Mara joked, leaning across the aisle.

"No way." Chris shook a fist at him. "Think of your own idea."

Glen Johnson raised his hand and suggested a fund-raiser. "We could use the money to donate Newbery and Caldecott Award–winning books to libraries in underprivileged areas."

Mr. Cobb clapped his hands together. "Outstanding suggestion."

Noah Fein raised his hand. "They wouldn't have to be libraries. You could donate the books to homeless shelters or soup kitchens around the country."

"I like this," Mr. Cobb said, striding vigorously up and down the aisle between desks. "We're on a roll. Let's keep it coming." He paused in front of my desk and tapped the desktop. "Valerie — excuse me, Mallory? Anything percolating in your brain?"

I straightened in my seat. "What about organizing students to read for kids at Stoneybrook Elementary School?"

Mr. Cobb stared at me. "And?"

I shrugged. "And that's it. We could go over three times a week and read after school."

Chris Brooks, who sat in front of me, turned around. "That sounds more like an after-school activity than a project to promote great children's literature."

"But it *would* promote children's literature," I shot back. "The books would all be carefully chosen, though they wouldn't have to be New-bery or Caldecott winners. I think there are a lot of good books that haven't won awards."

"What's wrong with award winners?" San-dra Hart asked.

This was really slipping off the track.

"Nothing," I said in exasperation. "I just feel that an after-school reading program should have a wide variety of books."

Chris shook his head. "I don't know about that."

I wanted to hit Chris. I was pretty sure I'd read more award-winning books in the last six months than he'd read in his whole life. Now he was acting like he was an authority on chil-dren's literature.

I blew my bangs off my forehead and sighed heavily. "I think a reading program of *any* kind can help make kids interested in children's lit-erature."

Mr. Cobb tilted his head back and rubbed his chin. "Maybe. Maybe."

He didn't sound convinced. I slumped down in my seat and glared at the back of Mr. Cobb's head as he walked up the aisle.

I spent the rest of the class *not* participating in the discussion. I was still miffed that Chris and Mr. Cobb hadn't liked my idea. I was cer-tain it was a good one. I just wished I'd pre-sented it better.

Our class officers' meeting was held after Mr. Cobb's class, in the cafeteria. Sandra walked to it with me.

"Isn't Mr. Cobb's class fun?" she asked, waving to friends as we hurried down the main hall.

"Fun?" I raised an eyebrow. "I can think of fifty things more fun than Mr. Cobb's class. Going to the dentist is one of them."

Sandra cocked her head for a second, then giggled. "You're kidding, right?"

I rolled my eyes. "Maybe."

"I thought your idea about organizing students to read to kids at SES was a good one."

I stopped dead in the middle of the crowded hall and said, "You did? Then why were you against it in class?"

"*I* wasn't against it," Sandra said in surprise. "Chris Brooks was against it."

"You sounded like you were siding with Chris."

Sandra giggled and waved one hand. "I was just trying to help him out. He's a really cool guy."

"So?" I stood with my hands on my hips, blocking traffic.

Sandra leaned closer to me and whispered loudly, "If I'd spoken up in favor of your idea, Chris might have thought I was trying to argue with him. I didn't want to seem pushy."

I folded my arms across my chest. "So *Chris* can disagree and be cool. But if *you* disagree with an idea, you're pushy?"

Sandra looked over her shoulder. "Yeah, something like that," she murmured. "Let's face it, guys don't like girls who act too brainy."

"Hey, move it, will you?" a beefy eighth-grader said huffily. "The bell's gonna ring!"

Sandra looped her arm through mine and pulled me toward the cafeteria. "Come on, Mal, you're making a scene."

I let Sandra lead me into the lunchroom. Mostly because I was stunned at what I'd just heard. After my progress report, everyone had teased me about my straight A's. I wondered if people — boys in particular — thought I was too brainy.

I sure didn't feel that way lately. Especially in Mr. Cobb's class. I felt like a total idiot. I could barely put two words together.

I grabbed a tray and followed Sandra down the cafeteria line. I watched as she waved and called perky hellos to everyone she saw. She certainly was popular. No one would ever accuse her of acting too brainy.

Justin and Lisa had already staked out our lunch table and were halfway through the daily special: Sloppy Joes, featuring everybody's favorite — mystery meat.

Sandra had passed on the Sloppy Joes —
"too messy" — and had settled on a container
of yogurt and a diet cola.

"Okay, Mal, tell us what you learned from
the old sixth-grade minutes," Justin said as Sandra and I sat down. "Anything interesting?"

I was glad to have something other than my
disastrous class with Mr. Cobb to talk about. I
told them everything I knew about the sixth-
grade class from five years before.

"They raised one thousand dollars to pay for
furniture and supplies for the library's student
lounge," I explained.

"Wait a minute," Lisa said, pausing with her
fork halfway to her mouth. "What student
lounge?"

"That's my point," I said. "There isn't one."

"So where did the money go?" Justin asked.

"Yeah," Sandra echoed. "What happened to
it?"

I pointed my carrot stick at the group. "That
is what we need to find out. I think we should
do some sleuthing and see where it went."

Lisa set her milk carton down. "I'm with
Mallory. Money doesn't just disappear. Especially one thousand dollars. Somebody had to
have spent it. We should find out who that
somebody is."

Justin nodded his head slowly. "Maybe we
should."

"I don't know." Sandra twirled her spoon around and around in her yogurt. "Don't you think that would just make trouble?"

Justin shrugged. "Maybe it would, and maybe it wouldn't."

Sandra looked at me. "I don't like to make a big fuss about things. Why don't we just think about *our* fund-raiser and *our* money, and forget about what happened five years ago."

"But I can't forget about it," I said. "What if this year's class came up with a cause we really liked and worked hard to earn money for it — and then our money vanished. We'd be upset about it, wouldn't we?"

Sandra tucked her hair behind her ear. "Well, maybe. But . . ."

Justin put his hand on Sandra's arm. "We wouldn't be making a fuss," he explained. "We'd just be asking questions. What harm can a few questions do?"

Sandra blinked at Justin several times. "You really think we wouldn't end up in trouble?"

Justin shook his head. "Of course not."

The more I watched Sandra act like a wimp around Justin, the more I realized how much I *didn't* want to act that way.

"Then it's settled," I declared forcefully to the group. "We start our investigation on Monday."

Justin looked a little taken aback. But then he nodded. "Monday it is."

Weekends are usually a nice break from school. But not this one. I had a lot to think about. Mr. Cobb's class was my main worry. If he really was grading based on participation, then my straight-A average was about to be blown. Big time.

But it wasn't just the grade part that was upsetting. It was also the *me* part. How could I have turned into such a wimp?

It was almost as if I checked the *real* Mallory Pike at the door to Mr. Cobb's classroom and put on a different personality during his class. But why? Because Mr. Cobb was cute? Because I didn't want people to think I was a brain?

I thought about this all Friday night. And all day Saturday. That morning, Mom had asked me to keep an eye on Margo, Claire, and Nicky while she ran some errands. Vanessa was at a friend's house and the triplets are old enough to take care of themselves. I sat in the backyard, thinking about Mr. Cobb and watching my brother and sisters rehearse for the Memorial Day parade.

"Here's my drum." Claire proudly held up a baby-wipe box with construction paper taped across the top. She thumped on the paper and sang, "Pa-rump-a-pump. Pa-rump-a-pump!"

Nicky's drum was ten times the size of Claire's. It was a big box that hung from a belt draped around his neck. "This strap lets me march!" he declared.

Just to prove it, he marched in a circle, beating the box with an old wooden spoon. This was going to be some parade.

"No, that's not how you do it," Adam cried as he and the other triplets entered the backyard. They'd been down in the basement, decorating their drums.

Nicky stopped and his shoulders drooped. "What am I doing wrong?"

"You're not doing anything wrong," Adam said. "It's just that you're supposed to be a band. A band marches together. Margo and Claire, go up there and march with Nicky."

Margo and Claire followed Adam's orders and fell in line behind Nicky.

Then Adam turned to Byron and Jordan. "Why don't you guys lead?"

"Right, Coach!" Byron said with a salute. He trotted in front of Nicky. Jordan was beside him.

"We'll circle the yard drumming," Adam explained. "Then, when I blow the whistle, we'll double-time it."

"Double time?" Nicky asked, wide-eyed.

Adam grinned. "Yeah. That means we march twice as fast as before."

"Cool!" Margo cried.

Adam took his place at the front of the Pike Family Band. Then he picked up his whistle and blew it three times. "Ready?" he bellowed. "March!"

I wish I had a video of that practice. Claire and Margo, trying to drum and march at the same time, were adorable.

And Adam looked so confident leading the group.

I thought about me and my total *lack* of confidence in Mr. Cobb's class. Why was that? Chris Brooks and Robbie Mara and even Benny Ott were completely confident, shouting out answers at the top of their lungs. But they were all boys.

I wonder, I thought as I watched Adam bark orders and joke around with the rest of the family. *Is Adam so sure of himself because he's a boy?*

But why would boys be any more confident than girls?

Maybe, I thought sadly, *because boys have it easier than girls.*

CHAPTER 7

On Monday morning I began my investigation. I'd called Sandra Hart and asked her to meet me before school started. *Way* before.

We were standing outside the front doors of SMS when the school secretary arrived to open the building.

"My, you girls are early," Mrs. Downey said, flipping through her big ring of keys.

Sandra looked at me, and I explained, "We need to do some research."

Mrs. Downey blinked several times. "Research? Now?"

"For the sixth-grade fund-raising week," I continued.

"Oh? Is it that time already?" Mrs. Downey shook her head. "The years just whiz by."

The secretary let us into the school without any further questions. I waited until she'd gone into the front office and had flipped on the hallway lights. Then I led Sandra down a back corridor to a door marked NO ENTRY.

"We can't go in there," Sandra whispered.

"We have to," I whispered back. "The class minutes are kept in the library, but this door leads to the basement where the school's records are kept."

"But what if someone sees us?" Sandra checked nervously over her shoulder.

"The only person who would see us is Mrs. Downey, and she's in the front office," I replied. "Come on, Sandra, don't chicken out now."

"I'm not being a chicken." Sandra grabbed my arm and her nails dug into my skin. "I'm just being cautious."

I turned the doorknob. Luckily, it was unlocked. I flicked on the light switch to our right, but that didn't do much good. A dim bulb lit the stairwell.

At the bottom of the stairs was a heavy door. I pushed it opened.

"P.U.," Sandra said, wrinkling her nose. "What's that smell?"

"Mildew," I replied. "All basements smell this way. Now, come on. I think the filing cabinets are over here."

I'd been in the basement only once before, but I knew this was where SMS kept files from all the previous years.

"I don't like this at all," Sandra moaned as

we tiptoed across the dusty concrete floor toward a row of green metal file cabinets. "It's smelly, gross, and probably haunted."

"If we hurry," I said, "we can be out of here in ten minutes." I scanned the typed labels on the cabinet drawers. Each was dated and covered a period of three years.

Sandra was still clinging to my arm. She pointed to the cabinet second from the end. "I think that's the one we're looking for."

"Great," I said, pulling her to the cabinet. I slid open the drawer and groaned. "Uh-oh. This may take longer than I thought. This drawer is crammed with stuff."

Sandra peered over my shoulder. "Find the financial records. Don't worry about the library files or anything else. The financial records will tell you when the money was donated and what was done with it."

I looked at Sandra in surprise. She was smarter than she let on.

I flipped to the file marked FINANCES. As I pulled it out of the drawer, Sandra said, "Just to be on the safe side, grab the financial reports for the next two years. Maybe the money was spent the following year. Or the year after that."

"Good thinking," I said with an approving grin.

Sandra checked over her shoulder. "But

hurry, will you? I don't want a custodian to catch us. Mr. Halprin really doesn't like it when students ignore his NO ENTRY signs."

I tucked the files under my arm and slammed the drawer. "Let's take these to the library. We can look them over there and maybe pump a little information out of Mr. Counts at the same time." (Mr. Counts is the librarian.)

When we stuck our heads out from behind the basement door, the halls were already filling up. Lights were on in most of the classrooms and the doors were open as we made our way to the library.

Once inside, we worked fast.

Sandra is really good at math. She looked at all of those confusing figures and knew exactly what they meant. "My dad runs an accounting firm," she explained, scanning the reports. "I grew up with these graphs."

We were able to figure out that the money had been donated to the school. And the one thousand dollars *was* earmarked for the library's student lounge. But the following year's records revealed that the money had been put into the building maintenance fund.

Sandra tilted her head. "It looks as if that class's money went to repair the roof and repaint some classrooms."

"Whoa." I leaned back in my chair. "That's not what that class intended at all."

Sandra nodded. "I think this comes under the heading of misappropriation of funds."

I sat forward. "Gee, that sounds like some big government crime or something."

Sandra shrugged. "I don't know if this really was a crime. I mean, it just looks like the school needed to use the money someplace else."

I shook my head. "But that's not right. If that class had wanted to raise money to fix the roof, or paint a wall, they would have said so. It was supposed to be their decision, not the school's."

"Oh, Mallory, it all happened a long time ago." Sandra scooped up the records and put them back in their files. "We should probably just drop it."

I looked at Sandra in dismay. "How can you say that?"

"Because I told you, I don't like to make waves," Sandra replied, standing up and pushing her chair under the table. "It'll just call attention to us, and people will think we're dorks."

"Dorks?" I didn't like the sound of that. "But don't you think what the school did was wrong?"

"Of course," Sandra said. "But the money's been spent. We're not going to get it back. So let's just drop it, okay?" She looked up at the clock on the wall. "I need to fix my hair and go to my locker before class. I'll catch you later."

It was weird. As I watched Sandra leave the library, she seemed to alter her personality. She plastered on her big smile and sang out her extra-perky hello to everyone she met.

I looked down at the musty file. Maybe Sandra was right. Maybe it *was* stupid to try to stir up trouble. Some of the kids in Mr. Cobb's class already thought I was a dork. I didn't need to have the whole school agree with them.

That afternoon, I arrived late to the BSC meeting — again. I'd been trying to think of some cool project for Mr. Cobb's class. So far, I'd drawn a complete blank.

"That's twice in a little over a week," Kristy said sharply, as I shuffled to my place next to Jessi. "What's going on?"

If there was ever a perfect opportunity to tell my friends about my troubles with Mr. Cobb, this was it. I opened my mouth to speak but quickly closed it. What if they thought I was a big baby who worried too much about grades?

I was upset about a lot more than just grades. But how could I make them understand that? Lately, I hadn't been very good at expressing myself.

"I'm sorry," I told Kristy. "I'm just having an off week. I won't let it happen again."

Mary Anne was watching my face as I spoke. She asked quietly, "Is something the matter, Mal?"

I wanted to shift the focus off me, so I mentioned the sixth-grade fund-raising dilemma. I told my friends about reading the minutes from that other class and checking the school files.

"Those guys raised the most money of any class — one thousand dollars. And the school spent it. Not on the library's student lounge, as the school promised, but on building repairs."

"What!" Kristy gasped, leaning forward in her director's chair.

"That's terrible!" Jessi cried.

"I can't believe it," Claudia said. "That's . . . that's almost criminal."

"Sandra Hart called it a misappropriation of funds," I reported.

"And she's right," Stacey replied. "I think that's against the law."

Abby slammed her fist into her hand. "That sixth-grade class should sue!"

I'd expected a reaction, but not one this big. Every girl in that room was upset. Even quiet Mary Anne.

"Our sixth-grade class gave the school the trampoline," Mary Anne reminded the group. "We all voted to do that. Can you imagine how upset we'd be if we found out they'd spent the money on fixing the plumbing or carpeting the front office?"

"This is an outrage!" Kristy leaped to her

feet and faced me. "You're not going to let this just slide by, are you?"

All eyes were on me. I didn't have the nerve to say, "Yes, I am." Instead, I stammered, "W-well, I'm not really sure what to do about it."

"Call the principal!" Kristy ordered.

"No," Stacey cut in. "Call the newspaper."

"Call the police!" Abby shouted over everyone else. "And then call a lawyer!"

A tight knot formed in my stomach. I could barely speak up in Mr. Cobb's class. No way would I be able to confront all of those people.

Jessi spotted the miserable look on my face and patted my knee. "Don't worry, Mal," she said. "You won't have to do this alone. The whole sixth grade will be behind you."

"And so will the eighth grade," Kristy declared, raising a clenched fist. "This is a problem for the entire student body."

The knot in my stomach started to relax. Jessi was right. I wasn't going to have to fight this battle all by myself. I had friends to support me. I beamed at them all, the best friends a girl could hope to have.

With the BSC rallying behind me, I suddenly knew what I had to do.

CHAPTER 8

"We have to talk to the principal," I announced Tuesday morning.

I'd called another emergency meeting of the sixth-grade officers to discuss what Sandra and I had discovered. We were huddled in a circle beneath the big sycamore tree in front of SMS. "We need to demand that the funds for the student lounge be returned."

Justin raised an eyebrow. "Demand is a strong word. I don't know if Mr. Taylor will like that."

Normally, Justin's words would have made me back down, but not today. I kept thinking of my friends in the BSC. "I'm not the only person who feels this way," I explained. "A lot of kids are upset by this news."

"Mallory's right," Lisa Mannheim said. "Every year the sixth-graders nearly kill themselves trying to raise money for our school. It's a big deal for all of us, and it should be taken seriously."

Justin rubbed his chin. "I suppose we could talk to Mr. Taylor. I mean, he does at least owe us an explanation."

"He owes us more than that," I said defiantly. "He owes us that student lounge."

"Do we *all* have to talk to him?" Sandra asked. "I don't want Mr. Taylor to think we're ganging up on him."

"We're the class officers," Justin said firmly. "We were elected to be the voice of the sixth grade. The four of us should present a united front."

Five minutes later, we trooped into the principal's office to have a talk with Mr. Taylor.

He sat back in his chair with the tips of his fingers pressed together in front of him, listening. When I finished my report he leaned forward.

"I understand your concerns, Mallory," he said in his deep voice. "But unfortunately you're right. That money *was* spent on building repairs."

"Why?" Lisa asked. "When it was specifically earmarked for the student lounge."

"Because . . ." Mr. Taylor took a deep breath. "You may not remember it, Lisa, but that year we'd had a particularly harsh winter. The roof needed replacing, pipes had to be fixed. It was a tough decision, but we felt we needed the building repaired more than we needed to save for a student lounge in the library."

"But what about now?" I asked. "The repairs have been done. Couldn't the school create the lounge now?"

Mr. Taylor shook his head. "Costs have risen over the last five years. Even if we had that thousand now, we would need a whole lot more."

We left Mr. Taylor's office with slumped shoulders.

"Well, that's that, then." Sandra sighed. "I guess we should just forget the whole thing."

"No way!" Justin exclaimed. "The fact of the matter is, the school was not supposed to use that money for repairs. They were supposed to give it to the library for a student lounge. There has to be some way that we can convince them to give it back."

"Why don't we talk to Mr. Counts?" Lisa suggested. "He may be able to give us some advice."

Sandra started to protest, but I put my hand on her arm. "Listen, Sandra, this is really important. We're doing this not just for our class, but for every sixth-grader who follows us."

"Well . . . okay," said Sandra. And she grinned.

When we talked to Mr. Counts, he told us

that the library staff still wanted a student lounge. "The costs may have gone up," he admitted. "But maybe not as much as Mr. Taylor thinks."

A bell went off in my head. "You mean, if some extra money were contributed, say from *our* class, the library might still be able to have the lounge?"

Mr. Counts peered at me over the top of his reading glasses. "If we had the original thousand dollars plus your donation, I'd say it would be very doable."

Justin frowned. "No good. That thousand was spent five years ago."

"Yeah," I muttered. "It was *borrowed* from the sixth grade's donation."

"If it was borrowed, maybe it could be returned," Mr. Counts interjected. "The school maintains an account for situations like this. It can't be used for building maintenance. It's for special projects. It's called a discretionary fund."

Justin draped his arms over Lisa's and my shoulders. "I think we need to talk to Mr. Taylor again. Like right now."

We raced back to Mr. Taylor's office.

After some intense discussion, he finally agreed to draw money from the discretionary fund. "But you're going to have to raise the thousand first," he said, pointing a finger at the four of us. "Then SMS will match the money you raise, dollar for dollar."

My eyes grew huge. "You mean, two thousand dollars would go to the student lounge?"

He nodded. "If you raise the first thousand."

"Whoa," I whispered to the others. "That would make our class the biggest contributors in SMS history."

Justin touched my arm. "It's up to you, Mal. You're heading this year's fund-raiser. Do you think we can do it?"

I thought about the kids who'd signed up to work the booths for the coming week. They were hard workers and very enthusiastic.

I nodded my head confidently. "We can do it!"

I was still flying high when I walked to Mr. Cobb's class. We'd scored a major victory with Mr. Taylor, and Justin and the other officers were behind me one hundred percent. If all went well, the students at SMS would finally have a lounge in the library.

But the second I entered Mr. Cobb's room, my confidence seeped away. I was like a balloon, bright and cheery one second, and the next — limp, completely out of air.

"Dinosaurs!" Mr. Cobb pointed to a display of book covers on the side bulletin board and read a few of the titles out loud. *Dinosaurs and How They Lived, Dinosaur Discovery, Dinosaurs A to Z, Dinosaur Bob, Dinotopia.*" He turned to the class. "Why do kids go crazy for dinosaurs?"

My brothers and sisters love dinosaurs because they seem like big friendly monsters. But did I raise my hand to say that? No.

"Dinosaur books are definitely a boy thing," Benny Ott declared. "I don't think my sister has ever read one."

"When I was a kid that's *all* I would read," Robbie Mara added.

"Tyrannosaurus Rex was practically my first word," Glen Johnson joked.

My sisters have always liked stories about dinosaurs, so I don't think it's a *total* boy thing. But I didn't raise my hand to say that.

"I was a dinosaur fan," Mr. Cobb said with a chuckle. "My room was covered with posters of dinosaurs, and I must have put together fifteen plastic models of dinosaur skeletons."

"Last summer my little brother and I watched *Jurassic Park* four times in a row," Jimmy Bouloukos said.

"That was incredible!" Chris Brooks declared. "They looked so real, didn't they?"

I wanted to mention the Barney TV show as an example of the amazing popularity of dinosaurs with tiny children, but Mr. Cobb, Chris, and Jimmy seemed to be doing just fine without me.

"When do you think this dinosaur craze hits

boys?" Mr. Cobb asked, continuing the discussion.

Age two was my answer. All my brothers and sisters were fascinated with dinosaurs that early.

Mr. Cobb had moved to my row and was looking right at me. I should have spoken up, but I panicked. I dropped my pencil so he wouldn't call on me.

When I finally straightened up to a sitting position, Mr. Cobb had called on someone else.

That was the way the entire class went. Every time Mr. Cobb even glanced in my direction, I either dropped my pencil or rifled through my backpack. Anything to avoid having to speak.

When the class finally ended, I looped my pack over my shoulder and hurried toward the door. I hated spending any more time in that room than necessary.

Unfortunately, Mr. Cobb blocked my way. "Mallory, could I speak with you for a moment?" he asked, fixing me with those pale blue eyes.

"Um, sure."

He sat on the edge of one of the desks and said quietly, "I was wondering how you were doing."

How was I doing? In life? Great. In Mr. Cobb's class? Terrible. But I didn't tell him that.

Instead, I plastered a smile on my face. "Fine," I said in a cheery voice. "Just fine."

He cocked his head. "Because if there's anything you'd like to talk about, we could arrange to have a conference after school."

A conference! The last thing I needed was for Mr. Cobb to think I was having some sort of problem with his class.

"I'm doing great," I said. "I really don't think a conference is necessary."

I could just see it. I'd meet with Mr. Cobb and freeze up. Nothing intelligent would come out of my mouth, so he'd think I was an idiot — and there would go my straight-A average.

"Are you sure?" he asked again.

I nodded firmly. "Positive."

CHAPTER 9

On Wednesday afternoon, I watched the digital clock on Claudia's desk change from 5:29 to 5:30. The Baby-sitters Club meeting was officially starting, and I was officially on time. Even Kristy noticed it.

"This meeting is called to order," she declared, tapping her pencil like a gavel on the arm of Claudia's director's chair. "And as the first order of business, I would like to congratulate Mal for being early."

Everyone applauded and I blushed. (Of course.)

Then Jessi raised her hand. "And I'd like to congratulate Mal for talking to the principal."

Stacey, who was sitting on the bed, leaned over the side and gave me a high five. "What did Mr. Taylor say?"

"He said they would be willing to refund the money they used on building repairs if we could match it with our fund-raiser."

"Can you?" Mary Anne asked.

"We're sure going to try," I said with a grin.

Abby folded her arms across her chest and leaned back against Claud's dresser. "I have to hand it to you, Mal. You don't look the least bit worried. I'd be chewing my nails off."

"The fund-raiser should be easy. It's Mr. Cobb's class that's hard," I confessed.

"Mr. Cobb?" Mary Anne asked. "That new teacher?"

"The heartthrob?" Stacey added. "With the baby-blue eyes?"

"He's my Short Takes teacher," I explained.

"Lucky you," Stacey cried.

"Unlucky me." I groaned. "The class has been a disaster."

"No way!" Kristy gasped. "I thought Short Takes was focusing on children's literature this time around."

I nodded miserably.

"And isn't that, like, your favorite subject on the planet?" Stacey cut in.

"It was," I murmured. "Until I landed in Mr. Cobb's class."

I hadn't really planned to complain about the class — in fact, I'd been afraid to — but once the door was opened, it all just poured out of me. In between calls for sitting jobs, I told my friends everything.

"I know it must be my fault," I said. "But

nothing seems to go right in his class. Mr. Cobb is grading us on our participation, and I can barely put two words together."

"You're kidding," Claudia said.

"It doesn't help that several of the guys are major big-mouths," I continued. "They never raise their hands. They just shout out answers whenever they feel like it."

"Mr. Cobb lets them do that?" Mary Anne asked.

"Mr. Cobb thinks everything they say is *so* funny or *so* smart. You'd think the rest of us didn't exist."

"But why don't you speak up?" Kristy asked.

"Mr. Cobb hardly ever calls on me. The few times he has, I felt so rattled that I said stupid things."

"Are you the only one having a problem with his class?" Mary Anne asked.

"I'm not sure," I said. "I've noticed that Jen Corn and even Lisa Mannheim have to struggle to be heard. Whenever they talk, Chris Brooks or Robbie Mara cut in, as if the girls don't even exist."

Jessi leaned forward. "I heard Sandra Hart tell Wendy Loesser that she *loves* Mr. Cobb."

I rolled my eyes. "You should see how Sandra acts in his class. Like a total goon."

"What does she do?" Claudia asked, passing

around a bag of chocolate stars (for us) and a bag of pretzels (for Stacey).

"She never expresses her *own* opinion. She always waits to hear what Mr. Cobb or one of the guys says, and then she agrees with them."

Jessi frowned. "Sandra never used to be that way. What happened?"

I shrugged. "Sandra's decided that it's dorky to be smart. She thinks boys won't like her if she acts like a brain. So she just goes along with whatever they say in class."

Kristy wrinkled her nose. "That's terrible."

I leaned my head back against Claud's bed. "At least *she* talks in class. I used to try to speak up. But now I don't even raise my hand."

"Why?" Abby asked. "You're smart. You made straight A's on your progress report."

"That's part of the problem," I explained. "When word leaked out about my grades, people started teasing me, calling me a Know-it-all. So now, I'm afraid that if I do manage to give the right answer, people will think I'm showing off. But if I say the wrong answer, I'll look dumb. So I just don't say anything."

"That must be frustrating," Mary Anne murmured sympathetically.

"I feel so mixed up." I ran my hands through my hair. "I don't even know what I know anymore. But if I don't do something soon, I could fail this class."

"Fail!" Jessi gasped. "But Mal, you have a straight-A average."

"Had," I said. "I'm sure Mr. Cobb's class is going to blow everything."

"That's not right," Kristy cried.

"Mal, you can't let a couple of obnoxious boys intimidate you," Abby said, raising up on her knees. "You know how smart you are."

"You're in charge of the entire sixth-grade fund-raiser," Claudia said, patting me on the back. "That's a huge project."

"You discovered that accounting error from five years ago," Stacey added. "Only a clever detective could have figured that out."

"And only a real leader would have been able to talk Mr. Taylor into putting that money back into the library fund," Kristy said. "You did that, Mal, all by yourself."

Jessi draped her arm over my shoulders. "See? Everyone in this room thinks you're smart and clever and terrific. And so does the whole sixth grade. That's why we elected you class secretary."

It's amazing what a difference friends make. I'd walked into Claudia's room feeling like a loser. But my friends reminded me of things I already knew about myself. And now I felt like a winner again. I was grinning so hard my cheeks hurt.

Rrrring!

Luckily the phone rang before I got a swelled head.

Abby answered it with her own flair. "Babysitters Club, Abigail Stevenson at your service."

Abby listened for several seconds, nodding. Then she said, "One sitter for Saturday while you take Sari to the doctor. We'll call you right back, Mrs. Papadakis."

Mary Anne was ready with the record book when Abby hung up. "One sitter for two at once," Mary Anne said. "Let's see . . . Kristy and Claudia are available."

"Oops," Claudia said. "I forgot to tell you that I have an art class from one to five this Saturday."

Kristy pushed her baseball cap back on her head. "Then I'll take it. That will give me a chance to help Hannie and Linny practice for the parade."

"Speaking of the parade," Stacey said, raising one hand and wiggling her fingers, "I really think we should discuss this instrument thing."

Claudia nodded. "We had a blast making drums and our own weird instruments, but have you guys heard how they sound?"

Mary Anne winced. "Like a bunch of kids banging on Kleenex boxes."

"Well, that's what they are," Abby said with a shrug. "We can't change that."

Kristy drummed her pencil on the arm of her chair. "Maybe we can. We just need to be clever."

It's rare to hear silence at a Baby-sitters Club meeting, but this was one of those moments. Everyone was thinking hard.

I twisted a strand of hair around one finger and thought about all of the orchestras we'd formed at my house. Sometimes we blew through paper-towel tubes. Sometimes we actually played instruments like harmonicas or plastic ukeleles. And sometimes —

"I know!" I shrieked, breaking the silence. "Kazoos. We could give all of the kids kazoos!"

Everyone turned to stare at me.

"Kazoos are cheap and easy to play," I explained. "All you have to do is hum."

"Brilliant idea, Mal!" Abby cried, clapping her hands together. "The kids can hide them inside their cardboard instruments — "

"And make them sound like real instruments," Claudia finished.

Stacey fell back on the bed with one hand draped dramatically across her brow. "Saved by the Mal!"

Mary Anne giggled and flopped backward across Stacey, adding, "I thought we were going to have to die of embarrassment."

"But not anymore," Abby said, joining the heap. "The kids will actually play tunes."

Claudia took one look at the group on the bed and yelled, "Pile on Stacey!"

I thought Kristy would disapprove, but she was the first to leap. Then Claud. Then Jessi and me. Before we knew it, every member of the Baby-sitters Club was on Claudia's bed, giggling.

CHAPTER 10

Saturday

Hey, Kristy, what do you get when you give 7 kids 7 KAZOOS?

I don't know, Abby, what?

I know the answer.

What is it, Jessi?

You get 7 more kids wanting 7 more kazoos.

That's right. You get a crowd. Or at least that's what happened to us when we met for Saturday's marching band practice. . .

It was Kristy's big idea (surprise, surprise) to ask all the sitters to bring their charges to Brenner Field to practice for the Memorial Day parade.

"Do you have the kazoos?" Kristy called to Abby as they met by the big rock on the edge of the field.

"No." Abby was carrying Marnie Barrett on one hip and holding Suzi's hand while Buddy ran ahead of them. She set Marnie down on the ground. "I thought you had them."

Kristy folded her arms across her chest and spoke very deliberately. "No. You were supposed to pick up the kazoos at Stacey's house."

"Stacey wasn't home," Abby replied with a stiff smile. "I thought she must have given them to you."

Kristy and Abby have a habit of bumping heads. It may be because they are so much alike — athletic, outspoken, and *stubborn.*

"I have the kazoos," Jessi called from behind them.

She and Becca had ridden their bikes to the field. Squirt was in the baby seat attached to the back of Jessi's bike.

"Stacey had to go to three stores, but she was able to buy twenty with the funds from our treasury envelope," Jessi explained as she parked her bike and unbuckled her helmet.

"She was running late, so she dropped them at my house."

Kristy took the bag from Jessi and handed a kazoo to Hannie and one to Hannie's nine-year-old brother, Linny. "Here, hum a few bars of something."

Hannie, who is seven, thought hard for a second. Then she put the kazoo in her mouth and hummed "Twinkle, Twinkle, Little Star." Linny joined her.

Kristy raised an eyebrow. "Good humming, you two. But we need something a little perkier for our marching song."

"Okay." Linny lowered his kazoo and sang, "Be kind to your web-footed friends, for a duck may be somebody's mother — "

Abby snapped her fingers. "John Philip Sousa, right?"

Linny gave her a confused look. "It's Raffi."

"But Sousa wrote the song," Abby's twin sister, Anna, said as she joined the group. "It's really called 'The Stars and Stripes Forever.' "

Abby had decided that since they were going to have band practice, a musician should come along. So she had invited Anna to join them.

"It's the perfect marching song for a parade," Anna continued.

"Terrific!" Abby cried.

Kristy turned to the Papadakis kids. "Why don't you guys pass out the kazoos and teach

97

the song to the Barretts and the Ramseys?"

"I already know that song," Buddy replied, reaching into the paper sack and pulling out a blue kazoo for himself. Just to prove it, he played the first stanza.

"All right, Buddy," Abby said, giving him a high five. "This band is ready to tour!"

When everyone had received their kazoos, they began playing. Imagine seven kids humming seven different tunes.

Kristy covered her ears to shut out the buzzing. "They sound like a squadron of insects."

"It's the attack of the killer bees!" Abby giggled.

"What they need is a band leader," Anna said, picking up a stick from under the hedge. She cupped one hand around her mouth and shouted over the buzzing. "Everyone! Stand in front of me, please."

The kids clustered together in a tight group around Anna.

"Good listening," Anna complimented them. "Now, I'll sing the tune and you hum along with me. Watch my baton!"

Anna tapped her stick on the rock, the way a conductor taps a baton on a music stand. Then she counted. "One, two, ready, play!"

The kids started playing the tune and Kristy

slowly lowered her hands from her ears. "Say, that's not bad."

"Not bad?" Abby cried. "It's great. Now all we need to do is teach them to march."

"Marching's easy," Kristy declared. "You just raise your knees high and march left, right, left, right."

Abby shook her head. "No, it's right, left, right, left."

Kristy folded her arms stubbornly across her chest. "It's left foot first. In all of the army marching songs it's '*Left. Left. Left*, right, *left.*' "

Then, to everyone's amazement, Kristy marched smartly in a square around the group, barking like a drill sergeant. "I *left* my wife and forty-nine children to die of starvation with nothing but johnny cake *left. Left. Left*, right, *left.*"

Abby waved one hand and scoffed, "That's what they do in the military. In *real* marching they start with their right foot."

Kristy put her hands on her hips and repeated, "*Real* marching? What's real marching?"

Jessi, who had already broken up the kazoo argument, stepped between them. "I think we should do some dancing in this parade. That would be really nice."

Abby and Kristy made faces at Jessi.

"Dancing?" Abby repeated.

"With cardboard instruments and kazoos?" Kristy added.

Jessi shrugged. "It would be a little more interesting than just marching."

"Hey! What's going on?" Norman Hill shouted from across the field. He and his sister, Sara, were tossing a Frisbee at the far end of the grass.

"We're starting a marching band," Buddy answered. "Want to join?"

"Sure!" Norman, who is a little on the pudgy side, tucked the Frisbee under his arm and trotted toward the group.

"Hey, wait for me!" Sara cried. Sara is taller, older, and speedier. She passed Norman in two strides.

At the same time the Hills were crossing the field, Adam, Byron, and Jordan appeared.

"You guys can't practice without us," Adam declared. "We have the drums."

"That's right!" Jordan declared. "We'll lead the band."

Buddy Barrett raised his kazoo over his head and whooped, "The boys are the leaders!"

Hannie Papadakis didn't go for that at all. "No way!" she shouted. "Boys in the back."

"Yeah," Sara chimed in. "The drums are always in the back of marching bands."

Adam hopped onto the big rock. "Not in this band. We're the leaders!"

Becca Ramsey, who is usually soft-spoken, cupped her hands around her mouth and started chanting, "Girls lead the band. Girls lead the band."

Sara, Suzi Barrett, and Hannie joined her. Pretty soon, the air was filled with the very loud shouts of the girls against the boys.

"Time out, everybody!" Kristy leaped onto the rock next to Adam with her hands in a T formation. "This is no way to start practice."

Suddenly, Jessi started hopping up and down and announcing, "I know! I know!"

"You look like an out-of-control cheer-leader," Abby said, catching hold of Jessi's shoulders. "What are you jumping around for?"

"*Everyone* can be the leader," Jessi declared.

"Huh?" Buddy made a face at Adam. "I don't understand."

"That will be our choreography," Jessi continued excitedly. "We'll line up in rows, and each row will lead the band for one block — "

"I see," Abby cut in. "Then they'll peel off and march to the back, right?"

"Right!" Jessi nodded.

"So each row has a chance to be the leader!" Kristy concluded. "It's brilliant!"

Now Abby was bouncing up and down. "We can do funny marching tricks, like Parade Rest."

To demonstrate, Abby keeled over onto the ground and lay on her back, snoring loudly.

Anna shook her head and laughed. "That's one of Abby's all-time favorite tricks. Now she can finally use it."

"How about March Right?" Buddy cried. Then he demonstrated by marching on his right foot and dragging his left foot behind him.

"Or March Left." Kristy did the same movement starting with the other leg.

Suzi Barrett squealed, "This is going to be fun!"

Kristy, who had thought to bring her whistle (once a coach, always a coach), blew one shrill blast. "All right, marchers, line up in rows of three!"

For a second, it looked as if there was going to be an argument over who would be in the first row to lead the parade. But Abby flipped a coin, and Hannie won the toss.

Hannie, Suzi, and Becca were in the first row. They were followed by the triplets, who were followed by Buddy and the Hills, who were followed by Linny and Madeleine. Jessi, Squirt, and Marnie brought up the rear.

"Let's circle the field," Kristy cried, leaping

out in front of the group. "Watch Anna and listen to me!"

(She and Abby had flipped a coin, too. Kristy had won.)

Anna conducted the band, marching backward, while Kristy led the marchers, shouting, "Left! Left! Left, right, left."

The procession circled the field, humming into their kazoos. With their goofy cardboard instruments and kazoos that sounded like a thousand mosquitos, the band created quite a stir in the neighborhood.

Charlotte and Dr. Johanssen were out walking their schnauzer, Carrot, when Charlotte spotted the funny-looking parade. Charlotte's eight years old. "Can I join in?" she begged her mother. "Please?"

Dr. Johanssen nodded and grabbed Carrot's leash as Charlotte raced to find a place in the band. Abby passed her a kazoo, and Charlotte joined Linny and Madeleine without skipping a beat.

Logan, who had been playing catch with his five-year-old brother, jogged over to Kristy. "Can Hunter march, too?"

"Sure!" Kristy replied. "The more the merrier!"

Mom was driving my younger brothers and sisters back from shopping for summer clothes when they saw the parade. She pulled the station wagon to a stop at the edge of Brenner Field. The doors popped open and Nicky, Margo, Claire, and Vanessa dashed across the field.

Abby was distributing kazoos as fast as she could. "We just ran out of instruments," she called to Jessi. "Every time I blink my eyes, more kids magically appear."

"What should we do about it?" Jessi asked as they watched the now huge group take one more spin around Brenner Field.

"We can't say no to a kid who wants to join," Abby said, adjusting her glasses. "But if this band grows much larger, it'll be out of control."

Jessi nodded. "Let's not worry about it now. We still have one more week."

Abby crumpled up the now-empty paper bag. "One week to figure out what to do about the biggest marching non-band in Stoneybrook history."

CHAPTER 11

"Let the FUN-raising begin!" I declared
Monday morning as I stood next to the Hearts
and Flowers booth.

I wore a button that read, "Ask me about our
FUN-raiser!" and a painter's cap covered with
heart and flower decals and buttons (courtesy
of Claud, of course).

Our booth was a giant flower stall, which
we'd set up by the front entrance to SMS. The
shelves were lined with white plastic buckets
filled with fresh-cut carnations, all donated by
ZuZu's Petals, the flower shop in downtown
Stoneybrook.

Helen Gallway was in charge of the booth.
She was dressed in hot pink bike shorts and a
T-shirt with hearts and flowers painted on it in
pink puff paint. Helen was surrounded by
messengers all wearing the same uniform and
Rollerblades with helmets and kneepads.

"One dollar, and we'll messenger a flower or

valentine to the sweetheart of your choice," Helen announced through a megaphone.

Jessi was working as one of the messengers. She skated up beside me. "I've already delivered three roses to lockers and two valentines to homerooms, and school hasn't even started yet."

"Five dollars!" I exclaimed to the crowd milling around the booth. "We've made five dollars. Only nine-hundred and ninety-five dollars to go!"

Justin Price, who had come for the launch, whooped a loud cheer and stuck his fist in the air. I have to admit, that made me feel good. Sandra, on the other hand, stood off to one side, looking embarrassed by the commotion.

Logan Bruno stepped up to the booth, waving two dollar bills. "I'd like to send a heart *and* a flower," he drawled in his Southern accent.

"Mary Anne's going to be very happy!" I sang out, wiggling my eyebrows.

"Now, this is from a secret admirer, so don't tell Mary Anne a thing," Logan said with a wink.

I pretended to pull a zipper across my mouth. "My lips are sealed."

Alan Gray was next in line and he ordered ten valentines. "For ten of *my* secret admirers," he announced in a loud voice.

Jamie Sperling, who was also one of the messengers, skated by me and whispered, "Alan's probably sending all of those valentines to himself."

I giggled. The booth was a big hit. As word spread, the line for valentines and flowers stretched all the way out the front door.

Lisa Mannheim hurried to my side. "Maybe we'd better start another line to handle the crowd."

"Don't worry, Lisa," Laura Aronsen called. "It's under control." She waved her hearts-and-flowers cap above her head and yelled, "Hey, everybody, the second line forms here."

Ten more people raced to stand in front of Laura. All of them clutched dollar bills in their hands.

I spied Sandra Hart by the water fountain and hurried to join her. "Look at all that money!" I squealed, rubbing my hands to-gether. "We're going to be rich!"

Sandra glanced over both shoulders, then whispered, "Mal, don't act so silly. People will think you're weird."

I was feeling too excited to worry about what Sandra thought. I just crossed my eyes and whispered back, "I *am* weird, Sandra. Didn't you know that?"

"Mal!" Helen called from the crowded booth. "We're going to need a third line. Can you run it?"

I saluted, then jogged to the flower stall to join her. "At your service."

The FUN-raiser was off to a terrific start. Justin knew it. Lisa knew it. And I knew it. All day Monday I was beaming. Even in Mr. Cobb's class.

Monday's class focused on the enormously successful picture book *Goodnight Moon*, by Margaret Wise Brown.

"Almost every child's bookshelf has a copy of this perennial favorite," Mr. Cobb said, holding up the green-and-orange picture book. "How many of you have read this book, or had it read to you?"

I raised my hand. It was my favorite when I was a baby. And a favorite of every one of my brothers and sisters.

"What makes this book so popular?" Mr. Cobb pointed to Lisa Mannheim.

Lisa tapped her chin with her pencil. "Well . . ."

Mr. Cobb waited for a second, then turned to Bobby Gustavson. "Bobby? Why did you like this book?"

Bobby ran one hand through his hair, leaned back in his seat, and doodled on a piece of paper with his pen. Mr. Cobb waited patiently until finally Bobby said, "I guess I liked the pictures. I liked trying to find that little mouse."

Mr. Cobb nodded. "Uh-huh. So the book has an element of mystery or puzzle-solving in it. What else?"

I raised my hand, and so did several other people. Benny Ott, who was waving his arm like a flag, finally shouted, "I liked the way my mom would say 'moooooon.' " Benny, who insists he's going to be an actor some day, stretched out the word, so it sounded like he was mooing.

But Mr. Cobb didn't laugh. Instead, he nodded thoughtfully. "The words in the book can be very soothing. Especially the repetition of them. 'Goodnight, *moon*. Goodnight, cow jumping over the *moon*.' "

"I liked the picture on the wall of the rabbit fishing," Robbie Mara said without raising his hand.

Megan Armstrong waved her arm in front of Mr. Cobb.

"Yes, Megan," he said.

"That painting is from another one of Margaret Wise Brown's books," she pointed out. "It's called *The Runaway Bunny*."

"Also a very popular book," Mr. Cobb added.

My arm was growing tired from holding it in the air. And I was starting to forget why I'd even raised it. But finally Mr. Cobb called on me just before the break he always gave us.

"I read this book to my sister Claire," I told Mr. Cobb.

He smiled vaguely. "Uh-huh."

"And Claire likes to watch the way the hands on the clock change in each picture. I do, too."

Mr. Cobb nodded. "The light in the room alters on each page, also. Did you notice that?"

"Yeah," Chris Brooks answered for me. "And the moon also rises. You can see it through the window."

At class break, I walked with Lisa Mannheim to the bathroom. "Mr. Cobb didn't give you any time to answer his question," I commented to Lisa.

Lisa nodded and frowned. "And he waited forever for Bobby Gustavson to think of something to say."

"Mr. Cobb does that a lot, doesn't he?" I said, pushing open the bathroom door. I crossed to the mirror and pulled a brush out of my backpack. "He doesn't seem to give a girl any time to think, but he'll let the guys take all day to come up with an answer."

Lisa cocked her head. "You know, now that you mention it, he seems to call on the boys more than the girls."

"He doesn't always *call* on them," I said, running a brush through my hair. "Robbie

Mara and Benny Ott just shout out their answers whenever they feel like it. They never raise their hands."

"While we sit there with our arms politely raised." Lisa demonstrated in the mirror by holding her arm crooked at the elbow. "Sometimes I think my arm will fall off before Mr. Cobb calls on me."

I shoved my brush back into my pack. "I wonder if Mr. Cobb realizes that his class discussions are so one-sided. *Boy*-sided."

Lisa shrugged. "I don't know. I'd hate to think he was favoring the boys on purpose."

"Me, too."

But after we returned from break, I noticed that Mr. Cobb continued his pattern of calling on the boys more than the girls. He also kept on giving the boys more time to think of their answers. Lisa was paying attention to the pattern, too. During the rest of the hour, whenever Mr. Cobb favored a boy — which happened a lot — Lisa turned to me and raised her eyebrows.

I left the class feeling torn. On the one hand, it was a great relief to know I wasn't the only one Mr. Cobb was avoiding. On the other hand, I knew something should be done about his favoritism. But what? I needed to think about it.

The week continued. Our FUN-raisers were

going full speed ahead. Tuesday's T-shirt–painting booth was a success, but Wednesday's Slam Dunk Your Teacher! booth was a monster hit.

We set it up on the front lawn of the school, and Liz Cohen ran it. Here's how it worked: The "victim" sat on a hinged plank above a big plastic tub filled with water. A bull's-eye target extended out to one side. For one dollar, a student bought three chances to hit the target. A direct hit would drop the "victim" into the tub.

"Hit the target!" Liz instructed the crowd. She wore a yellow slicker over her bathing suit and big rubber boots. "Dunk the teacher. It's that simple."

Many of the teachers were good sports about being dunked. Mrs. Gonzalez, an eighth-grade science teacher, wore a flowered bathing cap and a scuba mask. She sat on the wooden plank and squealed loudly every time the target was hit and she was dumped into the pool.

Mr. De Young, the boys' gym teacher, wore a pair of swim trunks that showed off his muscular body. He shouted fake threats like, "Hit that target and you're toast!" which made everyone laugh.

But the all-time favorite was our assistant principal.

"Our next victim is Mr. Kingbridge!" Liz Cohen called through a Mr. Microphone that she'd brought from home. "Who would like to dunk our assistant principal?"

There was a stampede for the line. It seemed that the entire student body wanted to hurl softballs and dunk Mr. Kingbridge.

He was only scheduled for five minutes, but he stayed for fifteen. "I never realized I was so popular," Mr. Kingbridge cracked when he climbed out of the tub for the last time.

While Liz ran the booth, Lisa manned the cash box. Later, just before Mr. Cobb's class, Lisa grabbed me in the hall and waved a piece of paper in front of my face. I don't remember ever seeing her so excited.

"Mallory, we're going to make it!" she squealed, pointing to the slip of paper. "If we continue raising money at the rate we're going, we'll meet our goal!"

"Lisa, are you sure?" I looked over her shoulder at the figures she'd written on the paper. According to her records, we'd passed the five-hundred-dollar mark on Tuesday. "Wow!"

Lisa threw her arms around me and gave me a big hug. "And it's all because of you. Congratulations, Mal!"

"Hey, what's going on?" Justin Price called as he passed us in the hall.

I flashed him my biggest smile. "We're doing some early celebrating. It looks like we just might meet our goal!"

"All right!" Justin beamed. "Way to go, Mal!"

The bell rang while Lisa and I were still in the hall. But we didn't care. We were too happy. We confidently threw open the door and entered Mr. Cobb's classroom late.

Mr. Cobb was in his usual spot at the front, perched on the corner of his desk. He was surrounded by Robbie Mara, Chris Brooks, and Craig Avazian, who were all laughing and joking with him.

Two girls, Renee Johnson and Jen Corn, sat quietly in the front row, their hands folded on their desks. Mr. Cobb seemed unaware that they were even there.

In that instant, I knew what I had to do. I took a deep breath and mustered all my courage. Then I marched to the front of the room.

"Mr. Cobb?" I said, stepping between Craig and Robbie. "Remember that conference you suggested? I would like to make an appointment to talk to you."

Mr. Cobb blinked his eyes several times, then said, "Certainly, Val — "

"*Mal*lory," I corrected in a loud, clear voice. "Mallory Pike."

"Right. Mallory. Okay, Mallory," Mr. Cobb said, checking his desk calendar. "I'll see you here after lunch tomorrow."

As I walked back to my desk, I noticed Sandra Hart sitting across the aisle. She looked depressed. I patted her on the shoulder as I walked by. She looked up in surprise and her face brightened into a smile. As I slid into my seat, I made a silent vow to have a talk with Sandra, too.

CHAPTER 12

I was afraid that after the fun booths we'd had for the first three days of the week, a booth that only sold candy would be a letdown.

But it wasn't, because of Claudia Kishi, artiste extraordinaire.

I know Claud's a seventh-grader and shouldn't have been working on the sixth-grade FUN-raiser but we were stuck for an idea. So I had called her.

"Candy, huh?" There was a long pause. Then she said, "Why don't you try a Halloween theme and fill pumpkins with kids' favorite candies?"

That sounded good. Much better than putting out boxes with wrapped candy bars and Life Savers in them. But then came Claud's stroke of brilliance.

"You could call it Trick or Treat. Some of the pumpkins could be filled with candies and some with disgusting things like plastic spiders and worms."

"Then kids could pay to reach into a pumpkin," I chimed in. "Fifty cents per grab."

The Trick or Treat Booth was fun to make. Fiona McRae painted it to look like a picket fence with papier-mâché pumpkins perched on the posts. Each pumpkin had a Halloween design on it. There were skeletons, bats, ghosts — you name it.

The girls who worked the booth wore black "Elvira" witch costumes, with wigs of long black hair. The boys wore Dracula capes.

Sandra Hart and I sold candy during the lunch shift.

Woody Jefferson, a popular eighth-grader, appeared at our booth first with his friend Trevor Sandbourne. "Hey, Sandra, pick a pumpkin for me, will you?"

Sandra reached for the vampire pumpkin. "Here you go, Woody. This one's perfect for you."

Woody seemed pleased with Sandra's selection and shoved his hand into the pumpkin. He came out with a fist full of Gummi Bears, licorice bites, jawbreakers, and tiny candy bars.

Sandra picked the pumpkin with the tarantula for Trevor.

"If Trevor and I are vampires and tarantulas," Trevor asked Sandra, "what character are you?"

"Me?" Sandra pointed to herself and giggled shrilly. "I'm the witch."

Trevor, who is possibly the handsomest boy at SMS, fixed his dark, brooding eyes on Sandra and said, "No, really, which pumpkin would you choose?"

Sandra looked at the pumpkins on display and gestured toward the one with the small black cat. "I guess that would be me."

"A kitty?" Trevor smiled and nodded.

"Great booth!" Pete Black, the president of the eighth grade, said as he picked the skeleton pumpkin that was filled with worms and plastic eyeballs. "Did you two make the pumpkins?"

"Me?" Sandra pointed to herself again. "No way. Fiona McRae did it."

Sandra and I worked non-stop for the first half hour of lunch period. When there was finally a lull, I pulled up two chairs and said, "Sit down, Sandra. Let's take a break."

Sandra checked first to make sure no one was looking. Then she collapsed into her chair. "My shoes are killing me."

I looked at her feet. She was wearing shoes with clunky two-inch heels. "No wonder," I said. "You should have worn sneakers."

Sandra slipped off her shoe and rubbed her

foot. "I always wear heels. They make me look more feminine."

"Why do you need to be more feminine?" I asked.

Sandra shrugged. "Guys don't like girls who are jocks."

This was the moment. I didn't know how Sandra would take it but I just dived in.

"You know, Sandra, you're really smart. *And* you're cute," I said. "You shouldn't worry so much about what other people think about you."

Sandra blinked at me. "I don't."

"You're wearing shoes that hurt your feet just because you think boys want you to be more feminine," I pointed out.

"Oh, that." Sandra winced.

"And you told me you don't like to contradict Chris Brooks's or Robbie Mara's point of view because you don't want them to think you're pushy."

"Did I say that?" Now she really looked surprised.

I nodded. "And just a few minutes ago, you picked out the smallest and meekest animal to represent you."

"Well, I couldn't say I was a vampire," Sandra replied. "Or a spider. Those are guy things."

I raised one eyebrow. "Are they?"

"Well, no," Sandra said, with the wave of her hand. "But if I'd picked the Frankenstein — "

"Trevor might have thought you were being too strong," I finished for her. "Is that what you were going to say?"

Sandra looked down at the foot she was rubbing. "I guess."

"I think I remember you speaking up more in class," I said slowly. "And in life. I mean, that's why our class elected you vice-president." I paused for a long time and then asked, "Did something happen?"

Sandra raised her eyes to look at me. All trace of the perky mask was gone. Her green eyes looked tired and sad. "Ever since I became a class officer, I'm always in the spotlight," she murmured. "I feel like the girls and boys in this school are watching me, waiting for me to slip up."

"Slip up?" I repeated.

"You know. Say or do the wrong thing," she explained. "If I don't have a smile plastered on my face every second I'm in school, people think I'm stuck-up. If I raise my hand too much in class, people think I'm a show-off."

Sandra's words hit home, which surprised me. "I think I know what you mean," I said. "When everybody started teasing me about the A's on my progress report, I felt like I was in the spotlight, too. And I really didn't like it."

Sandra pursed her lips. "Sometimes I think I would do anything to keep the attention away from me."

The next rush of students appeared at our booth as the seventh-graders were released for lunch. "Let's talk more about this later," I said as Sandra unbuckled her other shoe and tucked it under her chair. She worked the rest of the half hour in her stocking feet. (One small step, as they say . . .)

I went directly from my talk with Sandra to my conference with Mr. Cobb.

As I approached his classroom, my stomach started doing flip-flops. My throat went dry and my hands started to quiver. Not a good sign.

"Come on, Mal," I whispered to myself. "Get a grip."

I knew this talk was something I had to do — for me and for the rest of the girls in my class.

Mr. Cobb was sitting behind his desk, eating a sandwich, when I opened the door.

"Are you having lunch?" I said, backing up. "Maybe I should come back later."

"No, no." He gestured for me to come in. "It doesn't bother me, if it doesn't bother you."

I walked down the aisle and sat at the desk in front of his. I clasped my hands tightly in front of me and dug my nails into my skin. If I was going to have this talk, I needed to stop shaking.

Mr. Cobb took the last bite of his sandwich and wiped his mouth with a napkin. "I'm glad you came in to chat," he began. "I was starting to be a little concerned about your lack of participation in our class."

"That's what I wanted to talk to you about," I said, taking a shaky breath. "My reasons for not participating."

"You have specific reasons?" he asked, tossing his lunch sack in the wastebasket beside his desk.

"I, um, guess you could, um, actually call them observations," I stammered. "You see, children's literature is my favorite subject."

"Uh-huh." Mr. Cobb leaned back in his chair with his hands behind his head. "And?"

"And, well, ever since this class began, I've been unable to join in the discussions. For a number of reasons." I took another deep breath and continued. "One of them, I know, is my own lack of self-confidence about speaking out in this group. But there are other reasons." I cleared my throat and looked Mr. Cobb directly in the eye. "Reasons that involve you."

Mr. Cobb, who had been tilting his chair back, leaned forward abruptly. The two front legs of the chair made a loud clunk as they hit the floor. "Me? What have I done to you?"

"You haven't *done* anything to me, specifically. It's more what you *don't* do."

He folded his arms across his chest. This conference was going badly, I could tell. "And what don't I do?"

I ticked off my list of complaints (I noticed my hand wasn't shaking anymore). "You don't call on the girls. We raise our hands and you ignore us. And guys like Chris Brooks and Benny Ott, who never raise their hands, just shout out answers and you listen to them."

"Now, hold on," Mr. Cobb protested. "I call on girls. Just this morning, I remember calling on Megan Armstrong and Liz Cohen."

"Two really outspoken girls," I replied. "But do you remember calling on Jen Corn? I've watched her sit quietly with her arm in the air for fifteen minutes."

"What are you saying? That I favor boys over girls?" Mr. Cobb said. "Because that's simply not true."

"You may not do it on purpose," I said. My stomach, which had been flip-flopping, now turned into a big, hard knot. I continued anyway. "But you do it. Look at the time you give girls to answer a question. Maybe one second."

"You've been timing me?" Mr. Cobb's jaw dropped.

I wet my lips. "Well, yes," I said, looking down at my desk. "And you are very consistent. Girls have one or two seconds to respond to your questions. Boys, especially some of the guys you coach on the baseball team, take all the time in the world to think of answers. You let Chris Brooks think for nearly two minutes yesterday."

Mr. Cobb rubbed his hand across his face and frowned. Then he took a deep breath, choosing his words carefully. "Look, Mallory, a student has to take responsibility for herself. If you don't feel comfortable speaking out in class, you can't blame it on me."

"I'm not blaming you completely," I said, looking him in the eye again. "But I do think that the way you run this class has something to do with my inability to participate."

Unfortunately for Mr. Cobb and me, the bell rang. He pushed back his chair and stood up. "Well, thank you for coming to talk to me," he said stiffly. "I know it was probably difficult for you."

I nodded. "Very difficult."

"I can't say I agree with your observations," he added. "But I appreciate your feeling free to express yourself."

"Well, thank you for listening," I said awkwardly, standing up.

Luckily, several students — boys — filed into the classroom then and started chatting with Mr. Cobb. I stumbled out of the room and into the hall.

If I were to rate that conference on a scale of one to ten — ten being great and one being a disaster — I'd have to give it a two. Mr. Cobb hadn't yelled or thrown me out of the room, but I could see that he was more than a little miffed at me.

"Who needs straight A's anyway," I muttered as I walked home that afternoon. At least I'd had the nerve to speak up.

That night, I didn't worry about homework. I couldn't. I was too busy watching my brothers and sisters practice for the parade.

Margo insisted I sit on the couch and pretend to be the crowd. "We're going to march by you," she said in a very serious voice. "And when we do, you're supposed to wave."

"Yes, ma'am," I said.

The triplets took their position in front of the band with Adam yelling orders. "Claire, form a straighter line. Nicky, hold your kazoo with your elbows out to the side."

Byron spun and motioned everyone to back up. "Everybody, let's start in the dining room. We want Mal to hear us coming from far away."

"How far back should we go?" Claire asked. "If we start next door, it will sound really far away."

Adam chuckled. "No, the dining room will be fine."

As they disappeared into the dining room, I leaned back on the couch and sighed. A week ago, I thought my brothers had it easier than me because they were boys. But maybe they didn't.

All they had to do was lead a kazoo parade. *I* had to be a student in middle school.

CHAPTER 13

"Smile, babies!"

Mary Anne and Logan flashed big grins as Jessi pressed the button on her instant camera. They were standing behind larger-than-life cutouts of babies in diapers, poking their heads through the holes where the faces should be.

It was Friday, and Jessi was helping me run our Say Cheese! booth. My committee had made cardboard cutouts of babies, muscle men and tattooed women in bikinis, and punk rockers. And picture this, the local camera shop had donated the film. It was a smash hit!

We'd set up Say Cheese! stations all around the school, and each one had a long line of giggling kids waiting to have their pictures taken.

"Mallory!" Lisa Mannheim ran toward me waving a piece of paper. "We did it! We did it!"

"We reached our goal?" I gasped. "Already?"

It was only nine in the morning. We still had an entire day of fund-raising to go.

"There it is in black-and-white!" Lisa pointed to the figures on her piece of paper. She'd circled the number "one thousand" with bright red ink. "Anything we make today is gravy!"

Lisa hugged me. I hugged Jessi. Jessi hugged Mary Anne, who hugged Logan. It was another wave of hugging.

"Now that we have the student lounge," I told the group, "we can use the extra funds to decorate it."

"We could buy really fun posters," Jessi cut in excitedly.

"And big pillows," Benny Ott said, sticking his head over my shoulder. "For lounging around on and reading."

"Speaking of reading," I said, "we could use some of this money to buy new books for the library. And donate them in the name of all the students who worked on the FUN-raiser."

Lisa loved that idea, and gave me another hug to prove it. Then she raced down the hall to break the good news to Justin.

As Jessi and I reloaded our instant cameras, she said, "You should feel really proud, Mal. Because of you, our class was able to reach our goal."

I did feel proud. I think my face was stuck in a permanent grin.

Cokie Mason and Grace Blume (two of my least favorite people in eighth grade) were next in line to have their pictures taken. They paid their dollars, and while they argued over which cutout they wanted to pose with, I talked to Jessi.

"I feel like Dr. Jekyll and Mr. Hyde," I confessed in a whisper. "I spend half the day feeling really confident and smart. I spend the other half feeling intimidated and stupid."

"Are you talking about Mr. Cobb's class?" Jessi asked.

I nodded and checked my watch. "Which reminds me. Sometime before his class begins, I want to take a few minutes to review the book we'll be discussing today."

"We're ready!" Cokie called. She and Grace had chosen to pose as punk rockers (naturally).

"Say Grrrrr!" I clicked the button, then handed my camera to Jessi. "I'll see you at lunch!"

"Good luck, Mal!" Jessi called after me. "Remember, you're a winner!"

I tried to keep Jessi's words in my head later, as I hurried to Mr. Cobb's class. My conference with him had ended on a weird note. I hoped he hadn't stewed about it ever since and decided to take it out on me.

Mr. Cobb watched me come in and sit down. He even nodded hello to me, which he had never done before. After the bell rang, he cleared his throat and said, "*Animalia*, by Graeme Base. That's the book. Let's talk about it."

Jen Corn raised her hand. So did Megan Armstrong and Glen Johnson. Benny Ott shouted, "I think the pictures are great!"

"Graeme Base is a wonderful illustrator," Mr. Cobb agreed. He shot a nervous glance in my direction and added, "But in the future, Benny, raise your hand before you speak, will you?"

Chris Brooks's hand shot up in the air and Mr. Cobb started to call on him, then froze. He turned slowly to face Jen, whose arm was still up. "Jen?" he said. "You were first, I believe. What do you think of Graeme Base?"

Jen seemed surprised that she'd been called on and hesitated for a second.

"Me! Me!" Robbie Mara called.

Normally Mr. Cobb would have let Robbie cut in. But not today. He looked at me again, then said, "Hold your horses, Robbie. Jen is thinking."

Finally Jen spoke. She began quietly, but her voice grew stronger as she gained confidence. "*Animalia* is like one giant puzzle. First you read the book, just enjoying the pictures of the gorillas and the rhinoceroses. But gradually you realize there is a little boy hidden in each picture. So you go back to the beginning and examine each drawing, discovering more and more wonderful details as you go. It's a book that you can explore over and over again."

"Explore," Mr. Cobb repeated with delight. "I like that word, Jen. It's the perfect description of what happens when you open a Graeme Base book."

Jen, who had hardly been allowed to say a word since this Short Takes class began, seemed to bloom right in front of us. Her entire face lit up and she sat taller in her seat.

I think even Mr. Cobb noticed the change.

"My favorite Base book is *Eleventh Hour*," Robbie Mara declared from his seat. "When I was younger, I cut a bunch of the pictures out of the book and taped them to my wall."

"I did that with the L for Lions page from *Animalia*," Chris said. "But the lions gave my little brother nightmares so we had to take the picture down."

Mr. Cobb chuckled as he listened to them talk and added his own comments about how certain images can give you nightmares.

But then I saw Mr. Cobb realize with a start that several students had been sitting quietly with their hands raised, while he, Chris, and Robbie had chatted away. A frown creased his forehead.

Five minutes before class ended, Mr. Cobb took his place in front of our group. This time he didn't perch jauntily on the edge of his desk. He stood with his hands clasped in front of him, a serious expression on his face.

"I feel that I owe the entire class an apology," he began.

"What for?" Benny Ott called from the back of the room.

"For just that, Benny," Mr. Cobb replied. "For allowing some of you to shout out answers and for letting others sit too long with their hands politely raised without being recognized."

I don't think I breathed the entire time Mr. Cobb spoke. I was too amazed.

"It has been pointed out to me that sometimes I seem to favor the boys by allowing them more time to consider their answers to my questions and by encouraging them to shout out their answers. Today I realized that this is true. And I'm sorry."

I squeezed my eyes closed, hoping he wouldn't mention my name. He didn't.

"As you all know, I've just begun my journey as a teacher, and I want to make sure I fly right. I have the greatest respect for you and would never intentionally slight any of you. So if anything like this comes up again, please feel free to speak to me about it." He looked out at our class, pausing for a fraction of a second to smile at me. Then he added, "I'll try to be a good listener."

I could feel a lump forming in my throat. I was really touched that he had not only listened to what I had to say but had made a public vow to change things. Mr. Cobb was a good guy.

That afternoon, I joined Justin, Sandra, and Lisa in the front office. Four chairs had been arranged around the public address microphone. At 2:45 we were to make a joint announcement over the PA system.

Mr. Kingbridge spoke first. "May I have your attention. I am very pleased to introduce the officers of this year's sixth-grade class. They've proven to Mr. Taylor and me, and to all of the teachers at SMS, the power of positive thinking. We told them, 'We don't think you can do it,' and they said, 'Yes, we can! Just watch us!' "

As Mr. Kingbridge talked, the four of us exchanged huge grins. We really were a team. A very happy team.

"And now," Mr. Kingbridge continued, "I'd like to introduce Justin Price."

Justin leaned toward the microphone. "Hi, everybody. I'm sitting here with Mallory Pike, Sandra Hart, and Lisa Mannheim. We just wanted to share our good news with you. Lisa?"

Lisa's voice shook with excitement. "This year's sixth-grade fund-raiser, thanks to help from all of you, has brought in a grand total of one thousand, three hundred and fifty-two dollars."

"And that's an all-time SMS record," Sandra Hart added.

We could hear applause and cheers echo down the halls outside the office. Justin gave us a very enthusiastic thumbs-up.

Now it was my turn. I cleared my throat and tried to speak clearly. "The best news is, the money we raised is being matched by the school to pay for a new student lounge in the library."

Justin draped his arm over my shoulder as he spoke into the microphone. "How about that, guys? Let's hear it for Mr. Taylor and Mr. Kingbridge!"

Now we could hear loud whoops and whistles. Mr. Taylor was beaming.

After our announcement was over and the microphone had been turned off, Justin said, "What do you say we all go to Pizza Express and celebrate? We can invite some of our best volunteers and really pig out."

"Count me in," Lisa Mannheim said.

"Me, too," Sandra added.

Justin cocked his head. "How about you, Mal?"

I pursed my lips. On the one hand I really

would have loved to celebrate. But I still had a lot of work to do.

"I'd love to go," I said. "But I haven't even started my project for Mr. Cobb's class — "

"Forget that!" Justin cut in. "It's Friday! You don't have to do homework all the time."

"If I don't work on the project today," I explained, "I won't be able to work on it this weekend. I have a Baby-sitters Club meeting this afternoon and a big dinner out with my family at Pietro's. I'm baby-sitting all weekend and then I have to help with the Memorial Day parade on Monday."

"Okay." Justin shrugged. "Go ahead, be a brain. See if we care."

I winced. I hated being called a brain. But I had to stay strong. I knew if I didn't work on Mr. Cobb's project today, I'd never do it.

"*Other* people do their homework on the *weekend*," Justin teased. "But not *Mallory* — "

"Justin, cut it out," Sandra said bluntly. "If Mallory says she needs to do her homework today, then let her."

Justin looked startled. Sandra looked a little surprised herself. She turned and gave me a big smile. "We'll have a piece of pizza in your honor, Mal."

"Thanks, Sandra," I said, squeezing her hand. "And I promise to join you guys next time."

At 5:15 I was in my place in Claud's bedroom, anxiously waiting for the Baby-sitters Club meeting to begin. My tardy streak was over. Claud didn't mind my arriving early. In fact, we used the time to split an entire bag of Reese's Pieces.

"This meeting of the Baby-sitters Club is called to order," Kristy declared formally at five-thirty. "And as our first order of business, I would like to hear a full report from Mallory about . . ." She paused and grinned. "About everything!"

I took a deep breath and started talking. I went into great detail about the FUN-raiser, how much money we'd raised, and where the extra money would be spent. I told my friends about my agonizing conference with Mr. Cobb. And finally I told them about Mr. Cobb's apology to the class. They were very impressed.

When I finished with my news, Claudia was ready with a big plastic bottle of (sugar-free) punch. "I'd like to propose a toast," she said, passing little paper cups of punch to everyone in the circle. "To the very smart, extremely talented Mallory Pike."

"To Mal!" cried my friends.

CHAPTER 14

Memorial Day (I'll say!)

Next time I suggest we form a marching band, will someone please kick me? The Memorial Day parade was supposed to be a nice little parade with a few kids marching and playing kazoos. I would have to say it turned out to be a baby-sitter's worst nightmare!

Kristy had planned for the parents to bring their kids to the town hall half an hour before the parade started. No earlier. That way there would be enough baby-sitters to watch everybody.

The Barrett-DeWitts and the Papadakises had made arrangements with Kristy to come a little earlier. But the Hills, Newtons, and the Arnolds didn't bother to call anybody. They just dropped off their kids.

"Norman and Sara, you listen to Kristy," Mrs. Hill called from inside her car. "Your dad and I will be watching you from in front of the Rosebud Cafe."

"Okay, Mom!" Norman called as he and Sara clambered out onto the steps of the Town Hall. "See you later!"

Kristy was helping Suzi Barrett put on her google-blaster. She heard Norman talking to his mother, but by the time she stood up, Mrs. Hill had driven away.

"Wait!" Kristy called, waving her arms. But Mrs. Hill didn't see her.

"Did you want to tell my mom something?" Sara asked.

Kristy put her hands on her hips. "Yes. I wanted to tell her not to leave you here by yourselves."

"But we're not by ourselves," Sara replied. "We're with you."

"And so are we," two voices chimed in. It was the Arnold twins, Marilyn and Carolyn.

"What are you two doing here?" Kristy asked. "I didn't know you were coming!"

"We're going to march in the parade." Marilyn held up a kazoo. "See? We brought our own instruments."

"But I didn't plan for you guys. Where are your parents?"

Carolyn shrugged. "Beats me. We're supposed to stay with you until after the parade, and they'll come find us."

Kristy took a quick head count. There were six Barrett-DeWitts (Lindsey was with the Brownies), two Hills, two Papadakises, and now two Arnolds.

"Twelve kids!" Kristy groaned. "I can't watch twelve kids by myself."

"Thirteen," four-year-old Jamie Newton called from behind her.

"Jamie!" Kristy gasped. "I wasn't expecting you. Where's your mother?"

He pointed to a red van driving off behind Mrs. Hill's car. "I'm supposed to stay with you — "

"And she'll come get you after the parade," Kristy finished for him.

"Right." Jamie squinted one eye shut. "How did you know?"

Kristy shoved her baseball cap back on her head. "A little bird told me."

Marnie Barrett and Ryan DeWitt spotted a fat squirrel by the elm tree at the edge of the town hall's front lawn. They raced off trying to catch it.

"Marnie! Ryan!" Kristy shouted. "Come back here this instant."

They stopped in their tracks and turned back to look at her. "Why?" Marnie asked.

"Why?" Kristy gestured to the swarm of kids surrounding her. "Because there are thirteen of you and only one of me. We have to stay together. Or else."

"Or else what?" Jessi called as she hurried up the sidewalk to join Kristy. Becca and Squirt were at her side.

Kristy heaved a huge sigh of relief. "Oh, Jessi, thank goodness you came early. Look at this. I didn't know half these kids were coming. There's no way I can watch all of them."

"Don't look now," Jessi said, looking over Kristy's shoulder. "But there's more where those came from."

"What do you mean?" Kristy turned around and gasped as she watched my brothers and sisters march toward her. "Oh my gosh. We're up to twenty-two kids, and there are only two of us."

"Don't panic," I said, hurrying to catch up with my family. "I'm here. Now there are three sitters."

Kristy instructed all of the children to sit on the grass. "And don't move!" Then she turned to us and whispered, "What if more kids come? How will we keep track of them?"

"I don't know," I said. "But we'd better think of something quick, because I think those are the Hobart boys running across the park."

It's hard to miss James, Mathew, and Johnny. All of them have bright reddish-blond hair.

Kristy put her hands to her face and squeaked. "The Hobarts never told me they were going to be in the parade! This is getting completely out of hand."

"I'll say," Jessi said. "Mrs. Prezzioso just let Jenny out of her car."

We turned to watch four-year-old Jenny race to sit on the grass with the rest of the kids. Kristy, Jessi, and I frantically tried to signal Mrs. Prezzioso to stop, but she thought we were waving at her.

"See you back here," she called out with a cheerful beep of her horn. "After the parade."

Kristy stood with her arm frozen in the air. "I now officially declare this parade a disaster," she said in a shaky voice. "We need to call in reinforcements."

"I know Stacey and Claud are planning to join us thirty minutes before the parade starts," Jessi said. "But I think Mary Anne and Abby were just planning to watch."

"Well, they *can't*," Kristy snapped. "They have to help. *Everyone* has to help."

I spied a pay phone on the far corner of the town hall. "I'll call Mary Anne and Abby right now."

Kristy cupped her hands around her mouth. "Tell them to bring whistles."

"Whistles?" I repeated as I jogged backward toward the phone.

"Don't ask why," Kristy barked. "Just do it."

When Kristy is stressed out, she can be really bossy. This was one of those times.

"Why don't I have the kids practice their song?" Jessi suggested. "Then you can think."

"You do that," Kristy ordered. "And keep a close eye on the little ones. Make them sit in front of you."

"Right!" Jessi saluted.

Luckily for all of us, Stacey and Claud arrived earlier than they'd planned. Unfortunately, two more kids arrived with them — Charlotte Johanssen and Haley Braddock.

Now we had twenty-eight children and only five sitters. To make things worse, the staging area around the town hall was starting to fill up with other groups. The SHS marching band assembled across the street in the neighboring park, tuning their instruments. Several floats rumbled by as they made their way toward the front of the town hall.

The children seemed to take the bands and the floats in stride. But when the clowns appeared in their funny little cars, the children went berserk. They leaped to their feet. Several of the smaller ones raced to the curb.

"Candy!" Margo and Nicky shouted. "Throw us candy!"

They remembered past parades when the clowns had tossed wrapped candies into the crowd.

Jessi and Kristy ran to herd the children back onto the grass while Claudia and Stacey stopped the Hobart boys from leaping onto the clown cars.

Meanwhile, I was able to reach Mary Anne on the phone.

"She said she would grab every whistle she had in her house," I reported back to Kristy. "She also said to tell you she'd ask Sharon to swing by Pembroke's Party Store to pick up a few more." I took a quick breath. "She'll be here as soon as she can."

"What about Abby?" Kristy asked. "We need all hands on deck."

I grinned. "Abby was on her bike and out the door practically before we hung up."

Kristy checked her watch. "It'll take her about fifteen minutes to bike across town. Abby should just make it."

The next few minutes were nerve-wracking as Kristy paced back and forth in front of the band like a drill sergeant. Any time a kid made a move, she barked, "Back in your place. We need to stick together."

Two police officers rode up on motorcycles with their lights flashing. Then a woman with a clipboard spoke into a bullhorn. "I'm going to read off your names in the order that you will appear in the parade. When I call your group's name, please get in line."

"What's our name?" Kristy rasped to the group. "Buddy! What's the name of our band?"

Buddy didn't have the nerve to answer. He stared at the grass as the tips of his ears turned red. I recognized that sign and hurried to his side. "Just whisper it in my ear," I said.

But before he could whisper a word, the woman boomed over the bullhorn. "The Buddy Barrett Marching Band! Will the Buddy Barrett Marchers please line up next."

"Buddy Barrett?" Adam grumbled as thirty children scrambled to their feet. "Why isn't our name the Adam Pike Marching Band? I like that better."

"No time for that," Kristy barked. "Line up in rows of three, just like we practiced."

Some of the new arrivals had never practiced the marching maneuvers, so Jessi had to give them a quick lesson. She ran through the moves, showing them how to peel off and march to the back of the line.

Mary Anne arrived, waving a small plastic shopping bag. "I have ten whistles!"

"Great!" Kristy looped one around her neck and blew it hard. The blast was so shrill that several kids covered their ears.

"My plan might just work!" she declared.

"What plan?" Abby gasped, skidding her bike to a stop by the curb. Her face was red with exertion, and she could hardly catch her breath.

"Glad to see you could make it." Kristy grinned as she looped a whistle around Abby's neck. "Park your bike and I'll fill you in."

"Three minutes!" the lady with the bullhorn announced. "The parade will begin in three minutes."

"Three minutes!" Kristy gasped. "Huddle!"

Seven baby-sitters formed a tight huddle. Just like a quarterback, Kristy sketched out her plan for the parade in the dirt.

"Everyone take a whistle. We'll need two sitters marching in front, two on each side of the band, and three in the back. If any of the little kids break out of formation, blow your whistle. That will signal the other sitters that we've got a stray on our hands. Then herd them as quickly as possible to the back of the line."

"This sounds more like a cattle drive than a parade," Abby joked.

Kristy tugged on the brim of her baseball cap. "That's right, pardner," she drawled. "And we want to make sure every single little calf makes it to the end of this drive."

Then Kristy stood up. "This is one of our toughest assignments," she said. "The streets are going to be jammed with people. We can't take our eyes off these kids for a second."

We nodded solemnly.

"All right, then." She lifted her cap over her head as the parade music began, and waved it. "Let's head 'em up, and move 'em out!"

The parade passed by in a kind of blur. All I know is that the Buddy Barrett Marching Band was a huge hit with the onlookers. The kids must have played their kazoo tune at least fifty times. And each time the crowd went wild. All around us we could hear people cooing, "Look at those little kids. Aren't they darling?"

Several times one or two of the littlest kids would break away from the band and wander toward the crowd. But before they'd even gone five feet, a whistle would blow. Then one or two baby-sitters would go on kid alert and herd them back to the band.

After the parade was finally over and all the children had been returned to their parents, we collapsed, exhausted, on the front lawn of the town hall.

"Hey, you guys?" Kristy said as she lay on her back, staring up at the sky. "Next Memorial Day parade — what do you say we just watch?"

CHAPTER 15

The Short Takes course finally came to a close at the end of that week. I could hardly believe it was over.

I sat in class on Friday, watching Mr. Cobb hand back our final reports. After struggling with several different project ideas, I'd finally designed a reading plan for first through third grades. I'd stressed in my report the need for keeping a balance between "boy" books and "girl" books, and making sure that books from different cultures were represented.

"I've graded your reports," Mr. Cobb announced as he placed folders on each of our desks. "And written your grade for the whole course on the inside cover of your folder."

"Is it too late for a bribe?" Benny Ott cracked.

"It's never too late," Mr. Cobb quipped. "But I don't know if a bribe would help you, Benny."

"How about me, Coach?" Chris Brooks asked.

Mr. Cobb shook his head dramatically. "I'm afraid you're a lost cause, pal."

As I watched Mr. Cobb joke with my classmates, I thought about all that had happened since the course began. I wish I could say that after I talked with Mr. Cobb, I made a complete turnaround and was suddenly leading the discussions in my class. But that didn't happen.

I was glad I had found the courage to talk to my teacher. And Mr. Cobb really had made an effort to be fair this last week. But I was still hesitant about expressing my opinions in his class.

It's hard to admit this, but part of me was still afraid that people might think I was trying to be a brainy show-off, so I kept pretty quiet.

Mr. Cobb was now in my aisle. He held three folders in his hand. I could see my report on the bottom, the one with the red cover.

He passed Glen Johnson his report. Then he handed Bobby Gustavson his. Finally, Mr. Cobb turned to me. It was the moment I'd been dreading.

"Well, Mallory," Mr. Cobb said, still holding my report in his hand, "I must say, I was very impressed with this report. You did your research, and you seem to really know your children's literature."

My heart started thudding a little faster. From the way Mr. Cobb was talking, it sounded as though I had done really well. Could it be possible?

He placed my report on my desk. "Thanks. For the report — and for our talk."

Now my heart was really pounding and my throat was dry. I reached for the red cover. I hadn't done well in the participation department, but maybe my report had changed things.

I held my breath and flipped open the cover.

He had given me a . . . B+.

"Oh." I stared at the grade. My straight-A average was blown. I'd finally received a B. It didn't matter that it had a plus attached to it. It was a B. I took a deep breath.

"Aw, too bad," I heard Benny Ott moan from behind me.

I spun around, angry that he was making fun of my grade. But he wasn't. He was talking to himself. As I listened to the kids compare scores, I realized that Mr. Cobb had been a tough grader. Only two people had received A's.

"Can you believe it?" Lisa Mannheim caught up with me after class. "Mr. Cobb gave me an A!"

"You deserved it, Lisa," I said, genuinely meaning it.

"Thanks. How did you do?" Lisa asked.

"Mr. Cobb gave me a B-plus," I replied.

I could have been depressed but I wasn't. The past few weeks had been a learning experience. I looked down at my report and actually felt very proud. I'd worked hard for this grade. I had done my best.

And that's all that really mattered.

Dear Reader,

In *Don't Give Up, Mallory*, Mallory gets to take a class in children's literature, and she is very excited about it at first. I can see why. I have always loved children's books. I loved my own when I was a child, and even now I am always discovering new favorites. I like to browse in bookstores and libraries, and find interesting new books as well as stories I enjoyed when I was little. On my shelves are lots of the books I had when I was a child. They are well loved, and well read. I'm looking at the bookshelves in my office now and I can see my copies of *Mike Mulligan and His Steam Shovel*, *Chitty-Chitty Bang-Bang*, *Misty of Chincoteague*, *Blueberries for Sal*, *Pippi Longstocking*, *Beady Bear*, and lots of others.

One of the exciting things for me about being an author is getting to meet other authors. Over the years, I've been lucky enough to meet Judy Blume, Madeleine L'Engle, and R. L. Stine, among others. And one of my closest friends is Paula Danziger. In fact, we're writing a book together now. Books and reading have always been an important part of my life — just as they are for Mallory.

Happy reading,

Ann M. Martin

L. GODWIN

Ann M. Martin

About the Author

ANN MATTHEWS MARTIN was born on August 12, 1955. She grew up in Princeton, NJ, with her parents and her younger sister, Jane.

Although Ann used to be a teacher and then an editor of children's books, she's now a full-time writer. She gets the ideas for her books from many different places. Some are based on personal experiences. Others are based on childhood memories and feelings. Many are written about contemporary problems or events.

All of Ann's characters, even the members of the Baby-sitters Club, are made up. (So is Stoneybrook.) But many of her characters are based on real people. Sometimes Ann names her characters after people she knows, other times she chooses names she likes.

In addition to the Baby-sitters Club books, Ann Martin has written many other books for children. Her favorite is *Ten Kids, No Pets* because she loves big families and she loves animals. Her favorite Baby-sitters Club book is *Kristy's Big Day*. (By the way, Kristy is her favorite baby-sitter!)

Ann M. Martin now lives in New York with her cats, Gussie and Woody. Her hobbies are reading, sewing, and needlework — especially making clothes for children.

Notebook Pages

This Baby-sitters Club book belongs to ——————————.

I am ———— years old and in the ————————

grade.

The name of my school is —————————————.

I got this BSC book from —————————————.

I started reading it on ———————————— and

finished reading it on —————————————.

The place where I read most of this book is ——————.

My favorite part was when —————————————.

If I could change anything in the story, it might be the part when

—————————————————————————.

My favorite character in the Baby-sitters Club is ————.

The BSC member I am most like is ———————————

because —————————————————————.

If I could write a Baby-sitters Club book it would be about ——

—————————————————————————.

#108 Don't Give Up, Mallory

Mallory is very excited about studying picture books for her Short Takes class. My favorite picture book of all time is _____ _____ _____. My second favorite picture book is _____ _____ _____. If I were going to write a picture book, I would write about _____ _____. The main character would be named _____ and he or she would _____ _____. Even though Mallory loves picture books, she has a hard time in Short Takes because the teacher, Mr. Cobb, mostly calls on the boys. This is what I think of what Mr. Cobb does: _____ _____ _____. Mallory has the courage to talk to her friends and to Mr. Cobb about what he's doing. If my teacher were only calling on the boys in my class, I would _____ _____ _____. Always remember: don't give up!

MALLORY'S

Age 2 —
Already
a fan of
reading

Age 10 —
Still a fan.
Waiting to
meet my
favorite
author.

SCRAPBOOK

Two of my favorite things— babysitting and Ben.

My family— all ten of us!

Read all the books
about **Mallory**
in the Baby-sitters Club series
by Ann M. Martin

Look for #109

MARY ANNE TO THE RESCUE

Everyone in class stood up and started gabbing at once. I quickly made my way across the room toward Logan.

"Hi!" I said. "Are you all right?"

"Yeah," Logan replied. "Fine."

He sure didn't sound fine. His voice was soft and clipped. And he wasn't looking me in the eye. He just walked out into the hallway.

"Are you sure?" I persisted, following behind him.

"Um, let's go outside," Logan said. "I need to tell you something."

Now I was really worried. I did not like the sound of this.

Mary Anne?" Dawn's voice called from behind me.

I turned and said, "I have to talk to Logan. I'll try not to be long."

"No problem, take your time," Dawn called back. "I'll meet you back home."

Logan was already pushing his way through a side exit. I jogged after him. We emerged into the warm afternoon sunlight in an isolated corner of the Stoneybrook Community Center parking lot.

Logan slumped silently against the wall. His eyes were moist.

My heart was thumping like a jackhammer. I fought back tears. "What?" was all I could manage.

Logan swallowed deeply. A tear trickled down his cheek and he quickly turned and brushed it away, as if he were just scratching an itch.

Horrible thoughts shot through my brain.

He's seeing another girl.

A high school girl.

A college girl.

Maybe someone has died.

No, his family's moving. That has to be it.

My knees were shaking. I tried to look Logan in the eye, but tears were clouding the view.

"Mary Anne," he said, his voice cracking, "I need to tell you something very important. And you're not going to like it."

THE BABY-SITTERS CLUB®

100 (and more)
Reasons to Stay Friends Forever!

More titles... ▶

❏ MG48226-2	#82	**Jessi and the Troublemaker**	$3.99
❏ MG48235-1	#83	**Stacey vs. the BSC**	$3.50
❏ MG48228-9	#84	**Dawn and the School Spirit War**	$3.50
❏ MG48236-X	#85	**Claudi Kishi, Live from WSTO**	$3.50
❏ MG48227-0	#86	**Mary Anne and Camp BSC**	$3.50
❏ MG48237-8	#87	**Stacey and the Bad Girls**	$3.50
❏ MG22872-2	#88	**Farewell, Dawn**	$3.50
❏ MG22873-0	#89	**Kristy and the Dirty Diapers**	$3.50
❏ MG22874-9	#90	**Welcome to the BSC, Abby**	$3.99
❏ MG22875-1	#91	**Claudia and the First Thanksgiving**	$3.50
❏ MG22876-5	#92	**Mallory's Christmas Wish**	$3.50
❏ MG22877-3	#93	**Mary Anne and the Memory Garden**	$3.99
❏ MG22878-1	#94	**Stacey McGill, Super Sitter**	$3.99
❏ MG22879-X	#95	**Kristy + Bart = ?**	$3.99
❏ MG22880-3	#96	**Abby's Lucky Thirteen**	$3.99
❏ MG22881-1	#97	**Claudia and the World's Cutest Baby**	$3.99
❏ MG22882-X	#98	**Dawn and Too Many Sitters**	$3.99
❏ MG69205-4	#99	**Stacey's Broken Heart**	$3.99
❏ MG69206-2	#100	**Kristy's Worst Idea**	$3.99
❏ MG69207-0	#101	**Claudia Kishi, Middle School Dropout**	$3.99
❏ MG69208-9	#102	**Mary Anne and the Little Princess**	$3.99
❏ MG69209-7	#103	**Happy Holidays, Jessi**	$3.99
❏ MG45575-3		**Logan's Story Special Edition Readers' Request**	$3.25
❏ MG47118-X		**Logan Bruno, Boy Baby-sitter**	
		Special Edition Readers' Request	$3.50
❏ MG47756-0		**Shannon's Story Special Edition**	$3.50
❏ MG47686-6		**The Baby-sitters Club Guide to Baby-sitting**	$3.25
❏ MG47314-X		**The Baby-sitters Club Trivia and Puzzle Fun Book**	$2.50
❏ MG48400-1		**BSC Portrait Collection: Claudia's Book**	$3.50
❏ MG22864-1		**BSC Portrait Collection: Dawn's Book**	$3.50
❏ MG69181-3		**BSC Portrait Collection: Kristy's Book**	$3.99
❏ MG22865-X		**BSC Portrait Collection: Mary Anne's Book**	$3.99
❏ MG48399-4		**BSC Portrait Collection: Stacey's Book**	$3.50
❏ MG92713-2		**The Complete Guide to The Baby-sitters Club**	$4.95
❏ MG47151-1		**The Baby-sitters Club Chain Letter**	$14.95
❏ MG48295-5		**The Baby-sitters Club Secret Santa**	$14.95
❏ MG45074-3		**The Baby-sitters Club Notebook**	$2.50
❏ MG44783-1		**The Baby-sitters Club Postcard Book**	$4.95

Available wherever you buy books...or use this order form.

Scholastic Inc., P.O. Box 7502, 2931 E. McCarty Street, Jefferson City, MO 65102

Please send me the books I have checked above. I am enclosing $_____
(please add $2.00 to cover shipping and handling). Send check or money order–
no cash or C.O.D.s please.

Name_____ Birthdate_____

Address _____

City_____ State/Zip _____

BSC5962

THE BABY-SITTERS CLUB®

by Ann M. Martin

Collect and read these exciting BSC Super Specials, Mysteries, and Super Mysteries along with your favorite Baby-sitters Club books!

BSC Super Specials

❑ BBK44240-6	Baby-sitters on Board! Super Special #1	$3.95
❑ BBK44239-2	Baby-sitters' Summer Vacation Super Special #2	$3.95
❑ BBK43973-1	Baby-sitters' Winter Vacation Super Special #3	$3.95
❑ BBK42493-9	Baby-sitters' Island Adventure Super Special #4	$3.95
❑ BBK43575-2	California Girls! Super Special #5	$3.95
❑ BBK43576-0	New York, New York! Super Special #6	$4.50
❑ BBK44963-X	Snowbound! Super Special #7	$3.95
❑ BBK44962-X	Baby-sitters at Shadow Lake Super Special #8	$3.95
❑ BBK45661-X	Starring The Baby-sitters Club! Super Special #9	$3.95
❑ BBK45674-1	Sea City, Here We Come! Super Special #10	$3.95
❑ BBK47015-9	The Baby-sitters Remember Super Special #11	$3.95
❑ BBK48308-0	Here Come the Bridesmaids! Super Special #12	$3.95
❑ BBK22883-8	Aloha, Baby-sitters! Super Special #13	$4.50

BSC Mysteries

❑ BAI44084-5	#1 Stacey and the Missing Ring	$3.50
❑ BAI44085-3	#2 Beware Dawn!	$3.50
❑ BAI44799-8	#3 Mallory and the Ghost Cat	$3.50
❑ BAI44800-5	#4 Kristy and the Missing Child	$3.50
❑ BAI44801-3	#5 Mary Anne and the Secret in the Attic	$3.50
❑ BAI44961-3	#6 The Mystery at Claudia's House	$3.50
❑ BAI44960-5	#7 Dawn and the Disappearing Dogs	$3.50
❑ BAI44959-1	#8 Jessi and the Jewel Thieves	$3.50
❑ BAI44958-3	#9 Kristy and the Haunted Mansion	$3.50
❑ BAI45696-2	#10 Stacey and the Mystery Money	$3.50

More titles ➡

The Baby-sitters Club books continued...